Mary Teresa Maloney

The Legend of Nonnenwerth

and other poems

Mary Teresa Maloney

The Legend of Nonnenwerth
and other poems

ISBN/EAN: 9783337391058

Printed in Europe, USA, Canada, Australia, Japan

Cover: Foto ©Andreas Hilbeck / pixelio.de

More available books at **www.hansebooks.com**

THE LEGEND

OF

𝔑onnenwerth,

AND

OTHER POEMS.

By MARY T. MALONEY.

SAN JOSE, CAL..
J. J. OWEN, PRINTER.
1876.

PREFACE.

This book is published, like some others, not wholly for the public, but for a circle of admiring friends:—here let me include those whom I do not as yet know, as well as those who are my kind subscribers. Meanwhile having become a book, these poems will also reach that *ultima thule*, the hand of the critic, and let us hope considerate judgment will even then say:

> " The bard sighs forth a gentle episode
> And gravely tells—"

But in the opposite event, what if another Jeffrey should find—

> " His scribbling toils some recompense may meet,
> And raise this Daniel to the judgment seat "

The poems are the scattered amusements and impressions of years in Louisiana and California, except the Legend, which was commenced and completed as a front piece within the last few weeks, since mention was first made of the book, because Mr. Owen—that friend and patron of the Muse—said in a notice that the " Longest and best had never yet been published." I then tried to prepare something which might justify praise and expectation. It has been urged by some personal friends that I have chosen a subject for the principal poem of too old-time a character,—I may here answer that so did Sir Walter Scott; so did Tasso, and so did Tennyson of our own day, in his "Knights of the Round Table," or "Idyls of the King." I beg pardon of the last mentioned great poet who is yet alive, and might be provoked at one's comparisons.

When I had about half completed the Legend I was thoughtfully recollected of a strange coincidence: Mention is made in an appendix of Mr. Chorley's to a volume of "Letters and Memoirs," which he edited for Mrs. Hemans, that two of her "principal poems were unaccountably lost, or destroyed. One was entitled the 'Secret Tribunal,' and the other 'The Crusaders.'" He regrets them very much, and observes in his closing remarks, that if they ever should be discovered they would form the nucleus of a new volume of remains. The reader will perceive in the "Legend of Nonnenwerth" the suggestiveness of "Crusaders," and the author will modestly say, that knowing not of it till it was done, yet if she may have fulfilled in any wise the beautiful intention of one who has gone "before," she will be almost willing to resign the prestige of originality. M. T. MALONEY.

INDEX:

THE LEGEND OF NONNENWERTH.

TO DR. M. S. McMAHON THIS LEGEND IS DEDICATED, AS A

TRIBUTE OF ESTEEM AND GRATITUDE,

BY THE AUTHOR.

THE LEGEND OF NONNENWERTH.

[The Arch of Rolandseck only remains of the once strong and magnificent castle built by Roland, the nephew of Charlemagne. He chose for his site the pinnacle of Roderberg, overlooking the Rhine. From its watch-towers could also be seen the lake and convent of Nonnenwerth, in which its promised bride, believing him to be dead, immured herself previous to his long delayed return from the crusades.]—*Scenery of the Rhine.*

[Roland was the son of Milo, Count of Angiers, and Bertha, sister of Charlemagne. The word "Paladin," or "Palatine," afterward so common in poetry as a characteristic designation of the warriors of Charlemagne, was first applied to Roland and his followers by a Saxon poet who wrote in the reign of the Emperor Arnulphus, about seventy years after the death of Charles. In the deils of the Pyrenees is yet shown a flower called the Casque de Roland, and a steep and rugged defile in the Crest of the mountain is pointed out as the Breche de Roland. Here, also, in the last century stood a small chapel in the immediate neighborhood of Roncesvalles which tradition affirms to be the chief's resting place, who, together with Roland, comprising in all thirty nights of the Palace, fell victims to that memorable and treacherous attack of the Gascons. Thirty tombs without inscription were to be seen in the vicinity, and a quantity of bones were shown in a cave under the chapel. I have retained the precise identity of this spot though three others in the locality are pointed out and severally claimed as burial places of Roland. What earth is specially incorporated with the clay of the hero matters not and is probably unknown.]—*See Notes to the Life of Charlemagne.*

HY crumbling arch yet stands, O, Rolandseck!
 Far up the rocky steep of Drachenfels;
  There thrills the music of the streams that break
Their broad paths down to where the blue Rhine swells.
Cold are the craters of thy centuries,
Where Palatines have marched, thy paths are peace,
And thy green willows are yet dense in dells
Whence Charlemagne's gold banners and bright shields
Went forth to glorious strife on Syrian fields.

Fire-born the lava of thy seven heights;
Along the river castled turrets rise;
There clings the ivy on the tinted blights,
Soundless and luminous in evening skies.
Repose hath starlight and the mingling wave,
Decay hath sunlight and the voiceless grave,
While no clashed cimeter to shield replies;
No charger's footsteps near thy fountains fall,
No revels holdeth in thy roofless hall.

How shall we bring the records back, of days
Glad with the laugh and love and eyes of life?
The joyous brows that won their knightly bays?
The free, high worth of peace, the strength of strife?
The swan-like throats of music that have sung?
The deep vein'd, fine soft glances that have flung
Sweet souls into each other, and made rife
Their story with thine ages, freighted years,
So long gone hence with tributes and with tears?

Thy trees have fallen down to silent caves,
Thy floors of stone shut in the graves of men;
Rude piles make echoes from the troubled waves.
When winter night and storm return again.
These are of things not lost where Roland was.
Roland of crest and lance and bannered cross;
One of the kingly men who hath said to pain,
Thy tomb 's a beauteous toy, and lo! the stone
That rolls away from thee is called a crown!

＊   ＊   ＊   ＊   ＊   ＊   ＊   ＊

The crystal key of contemplation turns.
In the fine lock of auspices: create

With the old dust of time's uncovered urns
Blown sea-ward unto thee,* O, Golden Gate;
Not of thee, Shasta! high, unsullied peak;—
No records hath it, of thy light pure snow,
No armor-laden men, grown faint and weak,
There gladly lying down while life ebbed low.
Thy grand Columbian barriers n'er fell
Before th' invaders' footstep, and there lies
No shield or corselet buried in the swell
Of thy proud stainless waters, where they rise,
That like a quick steed, who abjures the spur,
Boundeth the rocks among on freedom's way,
Below the bending pine and swaying fir,
And the white feathery foam and dashing spray,
Down to the fields of wheat and valley grass,
Down to the widening shore past flowering meads.
No fierce Thermopylae soiled any pass
With vain, dead-hates of conquests or of greeds.

So we are glad, but as with deepening tone
Of low, sweet music, and of garlands flung
Before some pale, sad cortege, that alone
Threads a dark pathway, so have mourners sung.

The night had come, †Mons. Jovis under snow
And the high calm's illimitable glow
Of all the midnight heaven,—looked as when
Hannibal rested with his weary men

---

* "Blows with a perfume of songs and memories,
Blows from the capes of the past over sea to the bays of the
present,"   —*Swinburne's Hesperia.*

† Mons. Jovis was the ancient name of Mount St. Bernard.
A temple of Jupiter formerly occupied the site of the present
famous monastery.

Around the Temple, whose dark walls then leaned
Against the great acclivity, half screened
From the loud winds of Clusa,—while in sleep
All the still camp, whose onward march would sweep
O'er Lombard cities, a dread destiny,—
Verona's—Pavia's long held siege to be.

The King watched, when others slept, he thought
Of the high plans his future actions wrought.
And at the morn, Duke Bernard's armors came
Across St. Bernard's mount, and left its lasting name,
A grand reunion in the valley made,
Each equal glorious march, a toil repaid,
With Charles, the greatest monarch of the Franks.
Villages, castles, towns, along the banks
Of Alps and river on the path he went,
Rose, not with moan of grief, or heart's lament,—
Not as the despot on his rampant way,
Brought they the palm branch, and the rose and bay.
Nor were they sullen at Mons. Cinisus;
With anthems they met him, and raised the Holy Cross.

And here with greeting, ere he pitched his tent,
An Envoy of the East—most stately—sent
Loaded with presents, while eight cymbals played
The hour in which the King his audience made.
With brazen bells, and heralds near they came,—
Slowly, the long advance a host proclaim.
And standing, Haroun's envoy thus addsessed
The mighty Emperor of all the West:
"My voice, O, King, this hour is Haroun's will,
Not as to Christian, Hebrew, Moslem—still;
But to the worth of all thy famous deed,
This adulation is his gracious meed."

This said, his servants, drawing near, unrolled
Fine silks, and Talmas, made of cloth of gold:
A curious bronze clock, with little balls
That at each brief hour's end its signal calls,—
The twelve displayed, and finely gilt the whole,—
As of some magic life it seemed the soul.
And lastly, coming in slow, silent grace,—
The guards wide parted to make clear her place,—
A large white elephant—as wholly white
As late-bathed plumes of swans at early flight.
Ah! we can tell not of her perfect praise,
Taught of the sun's warm travel, all the ways,
Endearing things they said along the line.
She seemed to hear; and shed like beams of wine,
A wordless answer in her eyes and mien,—
A sacred symbol there among them seen.
And she had for a present, a great tent
On her soft shoulders, folded as she went.
And bearing this she knelt before the King,
That he might reach with hands the costly thing.
In colors fine embroidered, flower and bird,
And startled antelopes, a fleeing herd;
The slender spire and crescent's silver gleam,
Worked in its fabric, as in sleep a dream.
"This for thy war tent on the mount and plain,
O, King of all the Lombard's, Charlemagne!"
Thus ended the fair speech of the envoy.

The listening King was pleased. With quiet joy
He answered: "Tell your monarch of the East
That in our mutual heart I love him best.
He is as I,—he hath most rapid zeal,
And energy as bold as that I feel;—

Magnificent designs, and mind as free,
For these, most high regard, he holds, with me."
At this he turned; a Syrian monk came near:
"Sire, in thy favor wilt thou justly hear
The journey's plaint I make, since, sadly told,
Are seventy thousand dinars tax in gold
Each year at Bagdad; for a bonded sun,
In Syria, shines the tomb of Christ upon.
O! in the splendor of thy royal name,
State unto Haroun that 'tis cause of blame,
And for thy friendly care he will requite
Unto thy Christian sons this tribute's right."

With courteous words the monarch acquiesced,
And glancing o'er his knights in earnest quest,
Singled out Roland from the pageant throng
Among the beautiful most fair and strong;
Had he such heavy brows as though the stroke
Of Jove's long fallen bolt, lain there had broke;
While in the beauty of his grave lips' peace
Love turned itself as doth sweet sounds in seas;
Forward he came with radiance just subdued.
His was the fervor of that quiet mood,
As of the Spartans it is said, no sounds
Of drum or trumpet filled their battle grounds.
They needed not, to rouse their valor's will,
Aught but the touch of lyre or lute's sweet thrill.
With rested lance he bowed, touching the mane
Of his fine charger and arose again;
Then seemed the King to give command alone,
But much of tender pride its undertone:
"Canst thou, O, Roland, find Anselmo, and
With ninety Counts depart for Holy Land?

Tell the good priest that I such message send
As you have heard ere now, unto the end,--
This to the mighty Caliph: that he move
His heart of mercy, for my heart of love,
And give my Christian people, long denied,
The freedom of the gates where Christ hath died,
They were so long anticipated—stayed."
The days of journey with import arrayed,—
Each cavalier's proud grace, each lance in rest,
Plumed helmet, visor closed, cuirass on breast.
But while they gathered all, one rode apart,
Not least in valor, but sad at heart.
We shall know what he did, that ere he went
To make a sweet farewell, when skies were blent
With the late day's deep purple and red gold,
And from the fields the lambs go to their fold.
Almost inaudible his stepping steed
That bruised the dewy perfumes of the mead,—
Into the mountains rode he shortly then,
Where the dark cypress waved in every glen,
Each dun dread precipice in sombre calm
Held the grapes ripening, while ethereal balm,
With gifts of fire, as hearts with visions blending,
Fed them, even from rocks, on which they grew de-
    pending
Like webs in winter, rock to rock * enlaced.
O'er the basaltic walls the vine stems traced
Where green their garlands in the summer hung,

---

* In summer when the vines stre'ch their tendrils from rock
to rock, they look like green garlands arranged to ornament
the stern basaltic walls that hem in the waters of the Rhine,
and in winter when the vines and the soil are both of a dark
color, these artificial terraces look like spiders' webs hung one
above another across the angles of deserted edifices.—*The
Rhine and its Scenery.*

Along the eddying stream their leaves had flung,
Great terraces of gloom, or vernal sheen,
Above the winding river grandly seen.

*   *   *   *   *   *   *   \#   \#

A bridge across the Nahe near Bingen stands,
Beneath it soft waves over shining sands,
With many arches pillared grand and old,—
Onward from thence, the road to Neiburwald;
Here Roland lingering rode and hastened not,
In fancy listening to each fairy grot
Below the little stones whose murmurs made
Indefinite strange sounds that chainless strayed:—
These were the haunting Gnomes of Whisperthal,
And weirdly unto him their voices call;*
"Return, delay, O, Roland, do not pass,
The Lorch lies in the sun, Roland, alas;
All the dreamy day in cymar of gold,
The lurly maiden sits where cliffs are cold,
Swiftly her white hands in the sunset shine,
With gleaming golden comb and tresses fine,
Thou knowest well the lifted eyes that haunt
Her wond'rous manifold sweet thrilling chant;
Roland, return, delay, O, do not pass,
The sounding falls are near, Roland, alas!"

But soon to silvery beechwoods he had come,
Where summery bee and flower with wings and hum,
Changed the dread current of his thought's day dream,
A fading dim perception it did seem

* The Whisper, a small tributary of the river Rhine, regarded
by the inhabitants with awe, on account of its voiceful cadences.
The Stone of Lorch is not far from it, on which the Gnomes
are supposed to sacrifice young ladies unless they are rescued.

To an o'er anxious passion of forethought,
With hope, and fear, and tenderness, enwrought.
Ah! such, he mused, is the proud soul's disguise,
Who will admit, fate takes him by surprise;
And we are pleased with such imaginings,
To hold its wayward reins, to plume its wings,
Or out of long sweet sighs to charm a strain
For festal deep repeatings of such pain,
Some way to wear the soul, than it is worn,
Yet always seen the forehead, and the thorn,
"O, I shall see her weep for this I fear.
Thou, rose of fragrance, needeth not a tear,
Since dewfalls nightly to thy full heart come;
My father, dare I wish these lips were dumb.
That oft with clarion deeds thy names recalled,
How shrink they now at this sweet love appalled."

  * *   * * * * * *

Gone are thine ivied years, sad, lone and fleet,
And of their things long lost, the bowered seat,
Near a grey lintel where sat Hildegarde,
The lintel there is yet time stained and marred.
And all the lofty Keep of Ehrenfels;
A peasant guide walks there to-day, and tells
How many hundred years have made it old
In those dense oaken glooms of Neiburwald.

That freighted hour he feared, his footstep stayed
Short of the moonlight on the open glade.
Ah; but the interludes of thought's excess,
Some fervor held just close to consciousness,
Made Hildegarde perceive that he was near.
And straight she waited, listened, saw him clear.

Then hastening, but why state with any word,—
To those who've mourned, 'tis but anguish stirred,
To those who have not known it 'tis but fraught
In words, with meanings pale, like statues wrought.
Anticipating all, white stained tear lids,
Whose pride's supremacy the tear forbids:
"O, I had thought with lute and garlands, thou
Would'st come, beloved; not, alas, as now."
So near his restful shoulder,—timid,—yet
Only her white hand on it lightly set.
He kissed her with some quick, impulsive will,
And then she leaned her head down and was still.

* * * * * * * * *

O, shadowy vails foreboding, not revealed,
It breathed in his soft accents, and was sealed
In the firm, tearless glance of her dark eye,
The imposing calm's restraint of agony.
As those great slumbrous banks of Indian palm,
Are quiet near the coming of the sea.
Their deep roots in a reef's captivity,
While all the Monsoon's desert laden balm
With burning winds sweep over them utterly.

"My dear, when I am gone, beware, Hunald,
Along the Spanish march his deeds are told,
And of his kinsman, Lupo, too, beware,
He gave me once a troth, not free or fair."
"Yea, sweet," she said, "resigning thee I will
In all high faith's collectedness fulfill
Thy love's behest each day and hour I live,
While slow the long months pass, or long years grieve,
Yea, sweet, I am content through burning ill,
My soul hath its completeness: Love will fill

Th' immortal aisles of heaven, though this earth,
With sounding waves of sea, and clouds of dearth
Whelm all its quivering throbs, and never pour,
Upon its censor fires, one token more."

And in her eyes of gentle smilingness,
Some high resolve whose deep flush filled her heart,
As when the sunset on the sea grows less
To splendors gathered, ere it all depart.
Buoyant and transient were this charming force,
But for dominion of the mind's resource,
Whose pause of love these governed aspects bless,
With sweet contending powers and wielding will,
And some faint echo of the voice:—"Be still,"
Eternal starlight, and the trembling air,
Thou art alone forever, everywhere.

   *   *   *   *   *   *   *   *   *

The soft unfolding purple of the dawn
Beyond the misty mounts like some vast throne
Beyond the utmost hills, whose hamlets kept
The previous night late vigils, and now slept;
With day the files of burnished steel, and flame
All musical with movement and the name
Of fair Jerusalem; advance and flow
Like strong tides in deep unison—they go.

How in high reverence were there unfurled,
Bright banners faceward to the Eastern world;
Behind them silence and their parting tears,
Before them effort, and perhaps long years.

The green shore's murm'ring current and the close
Of each long weary day to eve's repose,

The ridge of rock, the story vale, the plain,
Some Gothic citadel, the vale again—
The straggling line of horse, the strongest few
Contending swift ahead for the first view,
Not easy to describe, the emotions throng
That fill the Christian breast when, after long
And toilsome journeying, the olive shade
Gives welcome on the slopes of Gihon's glade—
The pools of Gihon, where a King* was crowned
The Bard of Canticles—each storied mound
Commands the battlements that rise above
The long desired—the city of their love.
Jerusalem! Jerusalem! they said:
Not saying more, in transport's awe dismayed
Some wept for joy on each other's breast,
And some the sacred earth low kneeling press'd.

They entered by the Bethlehem gate at noon,
When parleying with the guards had ended soon,
And to the Latin Convent guests they came,
With letters heralding their august fame.

At early morn they passed the holy door,
Where the long tides of constant ages pour
Their trains of worshipers; the slab they kiss
Is under hanging lamps, and polished is
With fine and sacred keeping: waxen light
Of three large tapers, many feet in hight.
In front, and at the ends—the lustrous gleam.
Of that which lies below reflects each beam.

* Solomon.

There washed was, and annointed, they explain,
The glorious body of the Lord, when slain.

To other holy places Roland went,
And with him prayer and silence, 'til his tent
Was strapped for travel—to the Caliph's Court.
When at the Convent gate blew loud and short
A herald's bugle note. Behold! he said,
"Tis Haroun comes himself through Gihon's glade,
And glad, those Christian sons looked from their
     towers,
The royal traveler distant yet some hours
They saw; then hastening, a selected band
Went forth to meet him—Roland in command.
And lo! what silver sheen 'neath azure skies
Glitters resplendent before Roland's eyes ?
Can he believe his sense ? A pagan hand
Raising the Christian standard where they stand,
Its glorious model hung with garlands rare,
Shook a soft perfume on the summer air:
Two silver pendant chains together meet.
Where hang three golden keys. O, sign complete,*
Ye mean the ransom of your sacred gates—
Your bloodless glory upon Roland waits.
And Haroun knew, it seemed, ere all expres'd
The pledged, devoted care that filled his breast,
Yet will he linger 'til their camps rejoice—
Each marble margined fount with cascade voice
And shaded plat of olive will go hence
With him when they have known his every sense.

---

* Such was the impressive and princely gift of Haroun Al
Raschid to Charlemagne—the keys of the Holy City and the
Christian standard.

Yea, though a stranger; so his task was told,
And he departed from the lands grown old.

*   *   *   *   *   *   *   *   *

To follow far the paths of deadly war,
The strife of Catalonia, fierce Navarre;
To dream by campfires in the Cevennes,
O! home and Hildegarde—of Love and Peace,
"Yet shalt thou meet with Lupo, Roland, when
Dark are the Pyrenees in every glen;"
This said the King: "nor shall be hushed the sea
Till all his rash affirms of wrath with me
Are well fulfilled,—replete with dastard pain.
Ha; that he dares contend for Acquitaine."

*   *   *   *   *   *   *   *   *

Close ranged the spikes of iron pallisade,
And yet the narrow stream its pathway made
Down through the centre of the long defile,
Whose steep declivities reached o'er a mile.
Bold each sharp pinnacle—sublime and bluff,
Oppressed with grandeur, we behold enough.
A fortressed castle on the southern end,
Its narrow deep-set windows gleaming, send
Slant light into the darkness, weaving shapes,
Their hollow, muffled veils strange beauty drapes
Around the wild flowers and the mountain ash,
And where the torrents o'er their barriers dash.
All the high woods soon bristled into life—
They come!—the Gascons to the bloody strife.
Many, entangled in the fray, once calling
Defiance or farewell to friend or foe,   [falling
Swooned to the bottoms where the wrenched rock

Drowned their last struggles in the surge below.
The stream was red with battle, dark with death
And soundful with the pangs of parting breath—
A disentangled rest for foe and foe.

* * * * * * * * *

" Issem, hang helmets on the towers to-day,
Perchance some pilgrim hitherward may stray
In weariness to rest with palm and staff.
Thou art not mindful of their needs by half."
So speaking, Hildegarde in patient gloom
Looked from the lofty windows of her room,
And in her voice once sweetness all there was,
The tone most over-sweet grown querilous,
As of a falchion that is quivering thrown
Under the rider while the fight goes on.— [close,
And then she walked, with veil and shawl, wrapped
Breathing the wan mists as they slowly rose
Mid transient shadows of soft, heavy bloom,
That made her faithful thoughts see Roland's plume.
Albeit she did know th' engaging thought
Out of the splendor of her fancy wrought,
And, O, ye stars! if any feet have trod
Upon ye,—they were things she said to God.

He had not come that day, though now three years
Had canceled hope's reserves, and gathered fears.
Sometimes she wept, or with adjuring thrill,
Implored to weep; restraint weeps not at will.
Tears, where are you ? down in the deep heart's urn,
And coming singly to the lids that burn
With strained anguish?   Oh! thou hast a power—
The peace of a resigned and tender hour.

No Peri ever hailed thee, boon of earth!
With half the longing thy forbidden worth
Comes o'er the heart whose proud rebelling eyes
Would send thee back all hushed where bleeding lies
A craven mouth of grief beneath its wings—
The refuge of barbed years—a wounded thing.
He had not come; because a journey then
Meant passing like a dream,—returning, when
The long months filled to years, and the lone seas
Brought dimly back the sails of Hope and Peace.
The dust and lustre of wide plains at noon,
Made lingering rest, and shade, the traveler's boon,
And the devoted palmer's cloak and stave,
Might find his journey's end—or wayside grave.

There is a mountain shrine—St. Roch's—where
All sylvan grandeurs mingle with sweet prayer,
The beechwood's verdure and the fount and thorn,
Whose near white blossoms fall on breaths of morn,
All gay luxuriance whose genial breeze
Goes on the sunshine to the distant seas,
The sun's pure deeps of sapphire, and the fold
Of lambs all gather'd, ere its last ray's gold,—
With the rose folded eyelids of sweet tears,
The beautiful, once only, of the years,
There in the midst of those who offered vows
Knelt Hildegarde with gently shaded brows,
Over her pale hands bended to the rail,
Only as yet, her golden hair their veil,
Of late she whispered secret mournful things,
Touched with redundance of love's hidden springs:
"Lo! the Lamb lieth on the altar's stone,
And I, O God, am here with thee alone."

But we may tell, when she had waited long,
For pilgrim's tidings, or for minstrel's song,
O'er the far solitudes, subdued, and vast,
At last a day auspicious seemed;—at last,
A day!—it may be as an almond wand,
Where with sweet surprise, a flower is found,
Or, like th' Arabian bee who from a rose
Feeds,—then with venom, and not honey, goes
To sting to madness, on the Kamsin's wind,
When all the white, hot plains make gazing blind,
The long untrodden cliffs two travelers climbed,
When slow St. Roch's bell for vespers chimed,
Their quiet converse was most earnest toned,
Its whispered theme some subtle secret owned:
"You watch her, and sing lays, while I explain,"
Thus said the elder, "think of Acquitaine,
And let no pity of your soul arise
For wringing hands of hers, or tearful eyes."
His shoulder marked;* his shell medallioned hat,
Donned it, the pilgrim's garb; malice like that;
Lo! in his eye, a fierce and dull gray light;
Where sits the condor, bird of haughty flight,
On rugged Andes, o'er the Pampas plains,
Such is the spirit that such glance contains.
Under his cloak soft flowing, mailed and strong
Lithe limbs, and like the Torso, studied long,
Carved shoulders of fine mould and massive grace
These the dread beauties of his form and face.
The gates were reached, a horn's blast sped their call,
And welcome was tendered by the Seneschal,

---

* A scallop shell on the front of the broad brimmed hat, and
the red cross embroidered or braided on the left shoulder of
the cloak distinguished the returned pilgrim.

Effacing trace of tremblings, hope and fear,
With glad expectance;—what may she now hear.
So deemed the castle maiden as with haste
The banquet hall's full laden board she graced:
Then, eyes of furtive guile subdued their glance,
Looked down with seeming mild of pious trance,
Waiting the questions, that he knew would come,
And leaning half concealed in the warm gloom
Of the carved oaken mantle, whose great hearth
Threw o'er the festal board its genial mirth:—
"And hast thou come, O, pilgrim, from lands where
The lute, and lance, and corselet fall in prayer,
And foremost martyrs fruitless not,—while low
Their deep atoning hearts in torrents flow?
Is the dread crescent in ascendance yet,
And the red desert sun in triumph set,
Where the unaltered cross hath lowered stood
The share of sorrow, and the price of blood?
And hast thou seen him, severed long from me?
O, faithful journeyers of land and sea."
"Lady, the King's knight, Roland, I have seen,
Last, in the towers of Capitoline.
We two oft watched at night, when stars grew pale,
The fire-flies on the banks of Arno's vale,*
And listened to the dulcet chirping hums

---

* The banks of the Arno on either side are flanked by
plantations of the olive and vine, the deep blue green of
the former contrasting strikingly with the light verdure of
the vine leaves. They are planted in alternate rows; and the
intervening soil is frequently made to yield a crop of barley.
Towards evening we saw a few fireflies, but these beautiful
and remarkable insects do not appear to flourish in Europe as
in the East, where they convert the whole atmosphere into a
galaxy of twinkling stars. The cicada made a prodigious chirping by the road side: almost the whole way from Rome it kept
up an incessant noise, scarcely audible when the carriage was
in motion, but sufficient to stun the ear the moment of a halt.—
Notes of a Wanderer—W. F. Cumming, M. D.

Of the Cicada, in the barley blooms,
Where the dark olive and the bright pale vine,
Luxuriant, alternate, interwine;
Far he had come; his valiant mission o'er,
When at the Tiber's mouth a rested oar
Brought him late orders for a lengthened stay;
Stern, but devoted, was his calm dismay."

"I know," she whispered, "and a holier tie
His pain and peril thus doth sanctify."

"Brought him late orders," he continued, "now
Be strong, O, lady, I must tell thee how
Not with a vanquished eagle, he would come
Back to the hamlets of his mountain home."

"Be strong: O, yes! for I have chastened well
Ere while my heart's surmises—thou may'st tell
Th' the unfaltering deed,—if with his royal right
He died—then, *I have lived*, as infinite."

Let not repeatings of the guileful speech
Through all her anguish its whole meanings reach.
Roland *was* at Rome, that recorded day,
The shrines were robed, for it was blessed May,
In all the bannered streets the populace
Rode in dense splendor, 'twas a day of grace.
The "Greater Litany's" sweet, solemn close
By many chorists chanted, grandly rose,
Then the Chief Pontiff turned, and raised his hand
Tranquil in blessing or in mild command;--
'Twas never known, for through the line there came
In hurried breaths and flashing eyes of flame,
Wild cries of blood;—a panic seizing all,

For Paschal and Campulus, voices call,[*]
Turbulent, traversing each open space,
The lances' streamers flash, and interlace,
Hatred had slumbered, but it was not dead,
On unsuspecting kindness it had fed,
Too trusting Leo,—close—insatiate—
Arose its deadly cries,—"down!" "mutilate!"
With coward, trembling hands—for crime is fear—
They bore him prostrate: "Hold, ye dastards, hear;"
Roland's that voice;—they halt to hear him speak.
The glow of his quick wrath hath dyed his cheek:
"Ye that with sacrilege would quench the light
In those pale, bleeding brows, defend your right;
I come! conspirators, vengeful, I come—

[*] The hatred which Campulus and Paschal, the two disappointed aspirants to the Papacy had conceived against the more successful Leo, had slumbered, but was not extinct. The ecclesiastical situations held by the two factions of Romans and the favor with which they were regarded by the unsuspecting Leo himself, gave them many opportunities of revenge. They hoped by a mixture of boldness and art to escape the consequence of their crime. The moment they chose for the perpetration of their design was while the Pope, attended by all the clergy and followed by the populace, rode through a part of the city performing what they called the Greater Litany. Pascal and Campulus were placed close to the person of the Chief Pontiff, and are said to have received from him some new mark of kindness on that very morning. All passed tranquilly till the line of the procession approached the monastery of St. Stephen and St. Sylvester, and even then, the banners and crosses, the clerks and chorists which preceded were permitted to advance till suddenly as the higher clergy began to traverse the space before the building, armed men were seen mingling among the people. The march of the procession was obstructed. A panic seized both the populace and the clergy, all fled but Campulus, Pascal and their abettors, and Leo was left alone in the hands of the conspirators. The Pontiff was immediately assailed and cast upon the ground, and with eager and trembling hands—for crime is generally fearful—the traitors proceeded to attempt the extinction of his sight and the mutilation of his tongue. It is possible that the struggles of their unfortunate victim disappointed the strokes of the conspirators, and that his exhaustion from terror, exertion and loss of blood deceived them into the belief that they had more than accomplished their purpose; dispersing the moment the deed was committed, the chief conspirators left the apparently lifeless body of the prelate to be dragged into the monastery of St. Erasmus.—*See Life of Chalemagne by G. P. R. James, Esq.*

Say; are those pallid lips forever dumb;
These mute, mild lips, that called you brothers long,
There in the dust low lying for your wrong."
Scene that was terrible—men desperate,—
They dared not stop, sheathed in the heart of hate,
A moment;—and the glimmering dust arose
With ring of helmets, and with javelin blows.
There Roland's violet mantle floating high
Cleaved a free pathway where the foremost die.
"Match ye with this," he cried, "your plots of harm,"
And fast and true fell his decending arm,
As tremor of faint stars o'er fallen snow,
Shuddered the jeweled helm on his brow,
So damp with ardor's haste—so pale with zeal,
Appalling triumph!—this didst thou reveal.

The almost lifeless Leo then was borne
To St. Erasmus;—all the night till morn,
Each gallant enemy, and zealous friend,
Watched,—holding counsel,—life and death impend.
But ere three days had passed the King had come
With speed,—encamping near the walls of Rome:
There Roland's tendered sword, the first glad gift,
That charmed his smiling eyes, whose heavenward lift
At lighted altars o'er that sword austere,--
Yea, wept—in hallowed love, in pride and fear.

    *   *   *   *   *   *   *   *   *

Come back where never changed, the mists that hung
Moving like censors, that are softly swung
Upon the mountains, or like robes, and feet,
That it was said, are beautiful to meet,
Where Hildegarde with white enfolded hands
On her still lap there sitting,—and blue bands

Of soft silk ribbon on her shining hair,
That with her soulful eyes their radiance share,
Wholly endowed with contemplation's sense,
She felt that love was prayer—and prayer was love
    intense.
Dark was her soul, but like the falcon's flight,
That riseth startled from the dews of night,
Assuaging fear, with lofty thoughts like stars,
That even unto hallowed death unbars
All the sails burning and the bays like fire,
The sight of shore to the wrecked hope's desire,
Proverbial love!—thou 'rt known by many a name,
But thou didst come to her, with these thy claim.
In dreamlike harmony that had become,
Her full heart's patience as with laden hum,
On slumbrous summer winds, the voyager
Starts from the troubled rose with wings astir.
"Thy calm sweet sanctity, O, Nonnenswerth!
It is now the chosen peaceful spot on earth
Where I can bear to live," she musing said,
"O, I shall bind my brows as one lain dead,
Where thy majestic bells at eventide
Along the waters of the pure lake glide,
Thy chimes will seem to call, Roland! Roland!
Sentence and prophecy, I will understand,
Yea! like the watched dove, I will lift thee, thought,
Out of the realms that on earth are sought.
Eternal purpose! serene thou'lt be fulfilled
Forever irrevocable, strongly willed,
Nothing to expiate—sacrifice alone—
Love's truest offering when its will is done."

    *   *   *   *   *   *   *   *   *

Ah, me; the fleeting months whose veil was white,

No tender last reprieve did them delight,
Only the curving lines grew quivering deep,
Where citadels of feeling sloftly sleep,
On the lip's pure rose--the brow's Madonna grace--
With all that heaven may seek, and earth efface.

Alas! the return along the peopled shore   [more.
Of Roland--the sweet welcome he would meet no
Alas! for the day that on the breeze was borne
The blast rung sweet and loud from one clear horn;
Maidens were singing, with garlands they come,
But why there too were tears--why were stern lips
      dumb ?
Issem, whose answers were low, sad, and brief;
How can the deadly dread that words control,
Make molten bareness of life's one goal ?

          *   *   *   *   *   *   *   *   *

Like a statue beside his steed, he stood,
And felt if he'd die that hour, 'twere good,
Then low on the sable mane like lead,
Dropped the utter strength of his proud young head,
Let us--O, let us think, that *she* never knew
How truly he lived, and how fondly true.

          *   *   *   *   *   *   *   *   *

There was feast at the board, there was welcoming,
With the bards and the guests and the noble King,
But for one who had wandered out alone,
A minstrel chanted this low sweet tone:
          Never on earth
To meet any more, but to live apart,
With each passing day like a veil o'er the heart--

Oh, never to feel the exquisite soul
Like the bird set free to its windward goal.
            Never on earth!
            Never on earth!
Though the light go out of the west each day,
Full of harvested hours, and the season's May,
Coming and going a cycle between,
Dividing sad hearts and that which has been,—
            Never on earth!
            It might be yet
The change of a bitterness turning sweet.
A life with its greatest crown at your feet,
Might your dear hands fall in their own loved way;
Ah those lips are dumb, and those still eyes say
            We must forget,
            Living, as dead,—
Nay;—though never may come replies
To the faithful heart wearing only sighs,
Twilight shall fall into purple haze,
Mornings shall long fill their golden days,
            Forgetting not,
Though forever far, beyond portals pale,
A sworn abiding and sweet avail.
Forbodings are clear:—when hath hope not striven
            Forgetting not.
With the burning stars and his lonely mood.
The singer then left him,—understood.

    For he journeyed to pray at the shrines of Rome,
But builded that tower when again at home,
For they said she is given to God, my son;
To God,—be content,—let his will be done;
Nay; for we cannot,—*the veil is black.*

So he builded that tower when he journeyed back,
And the walls of Nonnenswerth still are seen
From Rodenberg's height where the turrets lean.
Nature, who deviates not her way,
Is still as she was in the olden day,
Still the rays of morn upon Rolanseck,
O'er the Lake of Nonnenwerth softly break,
And the windows of Nonnenwerth now grown old,
Are yet to be seen from that pinacle bold,
Where a faithful heart lived and wept alone,
In the anguish of time that is dead and gone.
Rascida Vallis, is far and fair,
And the Casque de Roland is blooming there.
When you gather its creamy and crimson bell,
Sit down, and hear what the maidens tell.
There's the Breche de Roland, its fissure is deep;
There's the Chapel, where long, he lieth asleep.

LAMENT OF LEONORA.

AN ANSWER TO THE "LAMENT OF TASSO."

[Published by request.]

ARGUMENT.

J. H. Wiffen, one of the best English biographers and translators of Tasso, disproves pointedly the many asseverations of Serassi, who wrote in politic deference to Maria Beatrice D' Este, wife of tne Arch Duke Ferdinand, of Austria. To the conventional and heartless prejudices of this lady the love of Lenora and Tasso was a theme altogether distasteful, and on having rehearsed to her an opera founded on a comedy of Goldoni's she had the name of Torquato Tasso changed to that of Lope de Vega, observing that *it was not very respectful to recall in the presence of a princess of the house of Este the name of Tasso—a man who had behaved so ill to that illustrious family.* This is indisputable proof, in connection with the words of another writer, "that Serassi seems throughout to be laboring with a secret, or a least with a persuasion, which he is at a loss to conceal. Our author, Whiffen, admits "How far Lenora corresponded to the ardent love of Tasso must ever remain an inscrutable mystery." He observes: "I am ready to believe that Lenora might be at all times on her guard to prevent the testimonies of her peculiar esteem from being remarked by the jealous Court in which she lived, and that she was often induced to call up a passing frown in order to baffle observation or to mitigate presumption, she must have been well aware of the precipice on which she stood in the indulgence of any marked partiality towards a dependent of the Court, when she had refused the hands of princes; when she called to mind the imprisonment in which her mother had been consigned on renouncing Catholicism and finally, Alphonso's pride of rank and bitter persecution of those who once in reality offended him. These remembrances, to say nothing of the prudential considerations suggested by womanly reserve must have induced her to act with extreme caution in bestowing her encouragements. As to the imputed indifference which the Princess is supposed to have exhibited for the misfortunes of Tasso, and the effort she made to obtain his liberty, with the conclusion that some would thence deduce that her heart was never interested in his behalf: "This," observes Foscolo, with great truth, "is one of the negative arguments founded on a hypothesis that may be easily destroyed by a thousand others equally plausible. Was not the Princess anxious to avoid her own ruin? In taking too warm an interest for the poet did she not risk destroying herself without saving him? A poet who dared to love a Princess of Este and a Princess who had encouraged him were, in the view of Italian statesmen, scandals which could not even be spoken by any without rendering them guilty of high treason. But on what grounds do these suppositions rest; what proofs are there that Leonora did not exert her utmost influence to lighten his calamities and terminate the horrors of his captivity, his continuance in prison? Nothing is more likely than that he, whose mind was rankling with resentment, whose bosom was proof alike to the pathetic appeals of the poet. and the entreaties of sovereign princes, would turn a deaf ear even to a sister's intercessions. That she did intercede for him I sufficiently clear from a remark in his Canzone to the Princesses "Chi mi guido"—What star guided me hither:

"And who, alas, when I for freedom grieved,
Promised me hope, yet still that hope deceived."

All the presumptions of probability and all the arguments of reason concur to answer, Leonora. Such are the opinions of Wiffen and of Foscolo, whom he quotes. Byron, also, who turned when at Ferrara with more interest to the prison cell of Tasso in the hospital of St. Anna than he did to the monument of Ariosto, seems to be convinced of Leonora's responsive love; even while he makes Tasso deprecate her reserve in the famous "Lament" he expresses the existence of some *secret hope* as witness the following:

"I told it not, I breathed it not: it was
Sufficient to itself—its own reward,
And if my eyes reveal'd it, they, alas!
Were punished by the silentness of thine;
And yet I did not venture to repine."

The italics are introduced in the present quoting to show Byron's accredited opinion that Tasso was *convinced in his secret hopes*, whatever may have been the expression of his discontent at the adversity of circumstances. And again, he makes Tasso say: "And thou, Leonora; thou who wert ashamed that such as I could love—*who blushed to hear—*." Byron in his researches of old Italian manuscripts and libraries had perhaps a better chance than either Wiffen or Foscolo of forming an opinion on this subject. In the above lines he expresses that *peculiar fear* which accompanies the responsive love of a woman so placed as Leonora, without which there would be *indifference* and not *love*, and in the presence of which there is love, *trembling and true*. Again. a few lines lower down, so sure does Tasso seem to be of Leonora's suffering in common with his own th t he incites Leonora to go and reproach her brother with their *mutual misery*—

"Go tell thy brother that my heart untamed
By grief, years of weariness, and it may be
A taint of that he would impute to me,
From long infection of a den like this.
Where the mind rots congenial with the abyss,
Adores thee still;—and add—that when the towers,
And battlements which guard his joyous hours,

Of banquet, dance, and revel, are forgot,
Or left untended in a dull repose,
This—this, shall be a consecrated spot.
But thou—when all that birth and beauty throws
Of magic round thee is extinct,—shalt have
One half the laurel that o'ershades my grave."

This prophecy is now incontrovertable, not less from the pen of Byron than from the sorrowful forethought of Tasso, and since so many have tendered sympathetic tribute to Tasso in this:—the following lines are in the same spirit inscribed by their author to the memory of Leonora of Este:

E thou at rest, where silence folds her wing,
　　My dove; in "clefts of rock," by strange seas
　　　broken;*
I speak or smile; I dream awhile, or sing,
　　And yet to thee, send never word, or token.

Say, love, they're censor fires, with lid upraised;
　　Or Druid wands, with mystic leaf, and meaning.
He was not spoken *to*, whom angels praised;
　　His throne is veiled, whereon are seraphs leaning.

But I will know thee; in the dreamy close
　　Of music, and the drench of water flowers,
And in the high dome's imperial repose,
　　When day is turning into twilight hours.
　　　And, oh, when sobs break on some midnight sleep,
　　　Then, love its tryst shall keep.

What though with pealing glory of renown
　　My dark bereavement yet should crowned be,
Still would I gaze far up to where thy throne
　　Is out of reach; oh, brow that beams on me,
　　　Some earthward angel's pinion widely spread,
　　　Its glory on thee shed.

* "My dove in 'he clefts of the rock, in the hollow places of the wall, show me thy face."—*Solomon's Canticles.*

Oh, tender eyes of rarely templed thought
  Avails it now to breathe o'er thee this pain,
Hath thy soul casements whose deep stillness caught
  The radiance of strange hours that pale and wane
    Till one might deem their marble chaplets not
    The flowers a sulptor wrought.

Speak, I would say to thee, but that I fear
  I could not bear this weight of yearning; then
Too dear thou should'st become, too doubly dear,
  And *such* a prince of woe, my Lord of men,
How could I bear it so?—this life apart,
  With but the voiceful linger of thy breath
On some chance hours—thine eyes fire all my heart,
  Till days are misery and love is death.

Alas! that I might say, make not this pain;
  My slumbrous soul is half contented now.
Think! the world's sentence would but call it "stain"—
  My kiss, too happy, on thy lover brow.
And yet, pride, falling from its stronger morn,
  Over an altar of false majesty,
Would dare in clustered roses any thorn,
  To pierce the wayward feet that strayed to thee.

   *   *   *   *   *   *   *   *   *

I do believe thee, Face, so kingly wise,
  Turned on me fondly, almost deified;
I do believe thee; raised are drooped eyes
  To question, if for this, was love denied—
To question, if for this, was Love long tried,
  That herein I may find it, changed, transposed,
Life's marvel doubted, till the wounded side
  All of its mystery and truth disclosed.

Deity, Doubt, Shame, Life—all stand confessed:
  Sorrow, so silent for its just reproof;
Faith's late sad surety, that had been thrice blessed,
  Had it believed, and trusting, stood aloof.
Speak to me, love.   Though silent, I adore thee;
  E'en when I do not lift mine eyes to meet
Thy looks, so veiled.   O, sacred shrine before me,
  Silence is peace—yet were assurance sweet.

Speak to me, then, when near me at some fall
  Of night, upon the lonely, lonely sea,
When thy dear presence is so near that all,
  Its majesty of stillness, shadeth me,
Till I could kneel, in my excess of feeling,
  And voiceless happiness, close to thy side,
For the dumb answer of the bliss, revealing,
  How I had hoped, and had not been denied.

    *   *   *   *   *   *   *   *   *

Oh, *I* would speak to *thee*, if that I might;
  Oh, wilt thou hear me, in this voiceless pain
I am alone; and the still pall of night
  Is over all things, and the deep low refrain
Of spirit music, on the wandering wind,
  Haunts earth's broken places, like thoughts of thee
Seeking for rest within my heart to find,
  Only the billows of a troubled sea.
Ah, dost thou make this sweet and heavy thought,
  For the heart most overweary, one deepest sigh,
That finds its echo mid the things unsought,
  Because of their deep dread; ah! mournfully

'Twill hover round thee ever,* a music made
   To thy soul's symphony, the unseen thrones
Of· heaven, their splendors burn and fade
   In lonely human hearts, with none to own;
Oh! that thou wert near me, that I might weep
   Upon thy bosom and be not afraid;
Oh, then methinks that I could calmly sleep,
   And yet, the very thought's with dread arrayed
And yet there is no Peace but in the still sweet deep
   Of thy gentlest eyes,—there fond fancy leads
And I am quiet, while time unbroken
   Wreaths me a garland till the moments glide
To where falls the real; and the beauteous token
   Is borne away, where I may see it never,
With the lost life beats of the heart's wild fever.

   *   *   *   *   *   *   *   *   *

Oh this is over me, as mystic sleep
   That is not earthly sleep, or earthly waking,
Where voices whisper soft, and dark eyes weep,
   And lips grow pearly o'er the heart's deep breaking
Though I have said forget me—it is well
   Though thou hast said forget me, as its knell
That we should never meet, and never part
   To risk that anguish, where a tide may swell
Its agony of waves to each o'er beating heart
   Full of thy deep, deep love are the waters wail
And so I fear not, though it mournful be,
   For in the mist that shrouds thee like a vail,

---

* No power in death could tear our names apart,
As none in life could rend thee from my heart.
Yes, Leonora, it shall be our fate
To be entwined forever—but too late
               —*Byron's Lament of Tasso.*

I see the fair hand raised o'er Gallilee;
   And then I know *he* said that this should be;
But when thy voice told me I should forget,
   And thy dear hand silenced hope's sweet key,
I hushed the thrill that murmured with regret
   And made my soul obey thee silently,
But oft it wakes with haunting voices fraught
   That whisper e'er of thee *"Forget me not."*

     *   *   *   *   *   *   *   *   *

Thou art not doomed to ever be forgot,
   Yet hast thou said to me a low good-by
With trembling words whose meaning was unsought
   Of the sweet spirit in thy heart, or eye,
And thou didst leave me with a lingering look
   Like that the soul doth make in varying dreams
Vainly to realize I am forsook,
   And yet I am remembered like the streams
That trill their mournful music on the ear,
   Listless lying where the woodland teems
With unblessed worlds of mysteries as fair
   As the peaceful soul of the dreamer lying there,
But I am happy, heavy though it be,
   To dwell on earth of thy dear love unblessed,
For haunting melodies do promise me
   A light in thy dear eyes I ne'er have guessed,
When all earth's shadows shall in quiet rest
   Morning and night upon each pulseless breast.

I dreamed of thee, methought a temple fair
   Was o'er us, and its lighted aisles were teeming,
And pale and sad thou wert standing there
   In a dense throng but to my fond eyes seeming

Noble in thy proud grace, as I know thou art,
  How trembled my glad heart in my dreaming.
Thou didst not see me, and I reached a dais
  On which stood others whom I did not know;
Soon fire swept round us, and the fearful blaze
  Undermined the frail timbers neath our feet,
Then came to thee sight of my danger, and the woe
  That swept thy fair brow,—to my heart was sweet;
No word passed thy lip;—a silent look
  Gave me all the meaning of its paleness,
But though the hope of life my heart forsook,
  Born of that hopelessness—thine acknowledged love,
That look of thine, death's joy, a life might never prove,
  I did not perish and I tried to win thee,
And rocked my feet upon the swaying pile,
  But many glided in the throng between thee
And where lone I stood, gazing down the aisle
My eyes still saw thy sweet lips' agony comprest
And I awoke still yearning to thy silent breast.

Why didst thou come before me with thy radiant brow?
  Blest were my eyes gazing on its light,
But weeping bitterly my heart's voice low
  Claimed from me some lost forgotten right,
I dare not think or feel what this may be,
  Life's hope, and death's indifference be there,
I dare not look in the abyss where lie
  Those two things;—gone were hope and prayer,
I could not see my God! for O, 1 fear,
  That is a cave rock bound which he forgot,
Where the mad surges lash the rocks so drear,
  That chaos dirges ever,—he is not.
Oh, I dare not listen, dismayed I turn away.

No rest! no rest! for hand, or foot, or heart,
Turmoil and strife must ever be their sway,
  I ask ye winds, which gains the victor's part,
Eternal life, or Lethe's unseen deep,
  You moan and moan, but still you answer not.
Still unrevealed that pale mystic sleep—
  Shall the heart's beatings be all then forgot,
Oh, no! I cannot give them up!—their poignant love
  Is all too torturing, to quivering sweet,
Their living wild unrest immortal prove
  The soul that makes the heart thus mildly beat.

Oh, I remember when my proud heart reigned
  Like an immortal dove within my breast,
But now long struggling, her heavy wing hath strained,
  Since o'er the waves, long sought;—no place of rest,
A passionate appeal I make to thee:
  Should that moment come, when all soul worn
The dark waters make come rushing over me.
  Oh give me death with that sweet peace whose morn
Will rise in unknown splendor o'er the sea,
  Hide me in its waves ere the night of scorn
Should set around me by one look from thee
  When my eyes close upon thy bosom's deep,
Oh! kiss them, forever; to eternal sleep!

      *   *   *   *   *   *   *   *   *

For thy love's sake, Tasso, for thy love's sake,
  And for the clos'd behests of waiting years,
Kept in the patience of a tried heart mourning,
  Under the arches of stalactite tears,

Think of me, darling, when thy soul's deep hushes
  Grow wakeful in the length of some slow hour
Between the midnight and the opal gushes,
  When the dawn pleads with night and day for power.

Think of me, dark, in the clime divided   [come,
  From spring and summer, where sweet tides ne'er
And say, Ah, me, sweet heart, from mine elided,
  I love you yet, my love, though grief is dumb,

When thou art silent; for the sharp precision
  Of catching some dear memory gliding by,
Perhaps; dear love, such is my hour of vision,
  Thy spirit comes so near, and says, "'Tis I."

Believe me, darling, when thy gladness, paling,
  Seems more than weary, like a mournful river,
The curse-born Eden of the unavailing
  Thinks of the gates again, where angels shiver.

Take them—the roses—on the lone heath blowing
  And put them where thy breast is warm and white,
And when they die there, love, thou may'st be knowing
  They're but sweet allegories of a blight.

Thou'lt find the passion of thy lips, which break
  Upon their leaves, and pulsing, beat apart
With thrills of thy soft breath, as when a lake
  Is stirr'd, as once you said, was stirr'd my heart.

Near where we stood, the dark full summer boughs
  Met over us in arches green and grand—
I was forgetful of the wasting glows
  That burned their life within thy cheek and hand.

Sweet censors! that no earth may gather from
   Their spirit meaning any fire of dust;
The stone was rolled away ere morning come,
   And watchers lie as dead before their trust.

What care that nothing shelters that lone head
   From falls of dew that damp each heavy tress,
Whose temples fail to coolness, that were fed,
   To fever by thy glances' tenderness.

My *feet* were in the *dust* that should be sere,
   Over that head, ere heard those words of thine,
How near *thy heart* was, yet, "He had not where
   To lay" it, who had *earth* and *heaven* for shrine.

What care then, if the barren surge were spread
   Over it, dirgeless, still, without thy voice,
To break the turbid waste where tempests shed
   Their wrath's vain triumph for that one sweet choice.

Mind me not; though my head may not any cover,
   From winds and stars, tell me no more, because
A soft, warm hand in seeming falleth over
   A forehead claimless; a dear hand of loss.

I dared its touch, *thy* hand, I reached for it,
   Fearing the glow, the pressure's deep strong thrill.
And yet, would God; it held me infinite,
   Through every pulsing tribute of Life's will.

Dayspring of dreams, burn oft for thee, and ever,
   It seems, as thou art bending o'er me, here,
Thy mouth's intense sweet sigh, its flush of fever,
   And, oh; the arms, that draw me, near and near.

Alas! wild dream; and heart of wild unrest,
   Loose life, I pray thee, from between thy throes,
My lover! oh, my lover! on thy breast,
   Pain, shame and rapture, could their bonds unclose.

Too well I know thee vain, deep kindling thought,
   In thy devotedness I'm doomed to be
Like to the coral fane that nereids wrought,
   A tempted labor, and an agony.

Forget me then, forget that tortured wail,
   That mirage of regret that rose afar,
For it the aisle of founts hath no avail,
   Nor plumes of peace, nor light of vesper star.

Take them away—an infinite sweet tone
   Keep thee till soft grass bendeth in the spring,
Over me lowly, light and windward blown,   [thing."
   Then say, "Dear head, thou'rt crowned with every-

Oh, be not sad; if never more again
   By soft-winged verse or sign thy love I move
Too much to weep, and suffer—its refrain
   "To suffer and to weep"—this were to love.

Too much of tears and strife were its dear cost,
   Till heart on heart their quest fall tremblingly,
To break, to beat, till heav'n and peace were lost;
   This cross is veiled, beloved! So let it be.

   *   *   *   *   *   *   *   *   *

Farewell, dearest! hush thy loving heart,
   Whose silver lyre is beating that bright shore,
Beyond my heart's low sigh, where deep winds start
   And bear the soft waves to the strand once more.

How can I bear it; all the dark, deep meaning
　　That droops beside thy spirit ?　Had it been
In the white flush of young life's bright beginning,
　　Ere blame had scorched it, or name called it sin,—

Thy soul's sweet whisper, through my being sweeping,
　　The anthem that on life is longest, deepest;
Oh, had it been before the time of weeping,
　　And ere this dumb regret its vigil keepest,—

How had my heart not stopped to fear or ponder.
　　How had it *then*, unbound, knelt at thine own,
Learning the colors in thine eyes' sweet wonder,
　　And gath'ring life's deep joy from one sweet tone.

How had I loved thee as thou should'st be loved;
　　How had I waited for each doubtful thrill,
That glance, or voice, or touch of thine had proved
　　Through all the glad life, at thy strong life's will.

How had the troublous heart o'erful with yearning,
　　Been given, beat by beat, beneath thy breast,—
A tide gone seaward, to its deep returning,
　　The while thine eyes, like stars, beheld me blest.

But hush, O heart, before the thought thou darest,
　　And count the links of chains and steps of time,
But do not count the heart beats, which thou fearest,
　　And do not call thy tenderest records crime.

VICTOR NOIR.

[The tragic death of this noble young Frenchman will be remembered, having occurred at the outbreak of the recent
Franco Prussian war. He was shot on the doorstep of a house
where he had just delivered a letter into the hands of Napoleon's nephew. The treacherous recipient thus taking the life
of his trustful visitor on the threshold of his own residence.
He was shortly to have been married to a beautiful and esti-
mable lady who in the midst of her own lamentable desolation
had to mercifully make her appearance on a balcony to quiet
the rage of the populace against his murderer.]

HIS breast was bared with its purple wound,
   And beneath his brow with a gleam profound,
   Like a Paynim lance, transfixed and bright,
Was the sign of his splendid soul's strong light;
   No shadow had fallen there.
It came, with the softness a hushed tread hath,
And voices suppressed from a vengeful wrath;
A pale light gleamed from a ladder's steep;
'Twas a simple omen whose tryst might keep,
   Far more than a people's prayer.

When on round upon round the heights they gain,—
There arose the chant of a sweet refrain,
'Twas the Marseillaise; on each lip 'twas loud,
For Victor Noir in his bloody shroud
       Lay dead in Paris that day;
And a child came near, that his eyes might see
How deadly the "hurt" in its majesty.
" Let me take his hand," said the tender child:
Strong hearts grew restless with anguish wild,
       And stern eyes turned away.

The people were roused, and many were armed,
Up to la Valleta the concourse swarmed,
Boys, with not a line on their temples' light;
Men's hearts surged hot, that might bleed that night,
       On the stones of a barricade.
Oh, not since the day that at Notre Dame,
The tri-color shone like an oriflamme;
On the tower's height o'er the startled guard,
It proclaimed that the danger was near and hard—
       Was there e'er such a scene displayed.

But lo! for her sake, in the sable, bowed,
With her lovely hair like an amber cloud,
Down by her sweet face, that was Parian pale,
Whose white calm brought o'er the angry wail,
       A hush, like a pulseless sea.
They parted each side, to a living aisle,
And the people stood for a weary while,
As they carried him slowly, like one asleep,
Their hearts so full that they could not weep:
       Thus they moved, all silently.

Two hundred thousand, along the street,
Yet their hearts pulsate with a single beat,
And the chant went slow where the mourners led,
To the quiet rest of the honored dead,
    With plume-draped funeral car.
Oh, the brother and friend, just heaven, hear:
" But yesterday he was so bright and dear,"
Strained hearts repeat, and the heaving throng
Bears the murmur on, full, deep and strong—
    "Vengeance for Victor Noir!"

Not banners, or stars, or lilies of France,
On the cortege gleamed from the long advance,
But they who bore him all loved him well.
And their burdened steps beat a measured knell,
    As they neared the wood of Boulogne.
And there, at the grave, with adjuring will,
From a heavenward eye and a sworn hand's thrill,
Like the stifled gush of a simoon's birth,
Was the murmur borne to the ends of earth,
    Make our vengeance, O God, thine own!

TORTESA AND MURILLO.

" Whosoever shall deny me before men."

[A story is told of Murillo which finely illustrates the power of truth and genius in sundering the bonds of adverse circumstances: Murillo had a mulatto slave, whom he employed in grinding his colors and performing the menial services of the studio. The students were sometimes annoyed at finding their work had been meddled with, when they entered the studio in the morning; and as the touches which their pictures received through the night were superior to their own, they superstitiously believed that some supernatural agency was at work, and they charged the mulatto, who slept in the studio, to keep strict watch. This he promised to do, but what was their surprise one morning on observing a head of Venus, which their master had left upon his easel unfinished, completely perfected, and in a style superior to anything Murillo had ever done. The master was astonished, and charged his pupils with meddling with his work. This they all positively denied; and poor Tortesa, the mulatto, was sternly commanded to tell all that had passed in the studio during his night-watchings. At first the terrified boy was silent, but at last he fell upon his knees, begged his master's pardon and confessed that the work was his own. He had heard the instructions given to the pupils, and profitted by them unobserved. In a moment the countenance of Murillo was changed, and lifting up the astonished boy, charged him to ask any favor, and it should be granted. Tortesa trembled, half doubting the sincerity of his master, but at last he found courage to say, "The liberty of my father." This was granted, but death early closed the career of him who gave such exalted evidence of genius.]

TORTESA ground the colors for Murillo;
   Tortesa was a boy, a gold mulatto;
A genius fervid as thy heart, O billow,
A tryst with thy forever, O Thallatta !

The students wearing robes made note, but lightly,
  Of him, his menial service, faithful all.
Fair days were passing and with sunsets brightly,
  Italian studios were beautiful.

For long the students wondered, in the morning,
  What hand with perfect touch, their pictures made
Superior! some grace of new adorning
  Put over like a star, where ONE was laid.

They said unto each other, something surely
  Worketh in watchful night with perfect skill,
This mystery! for done most fair and purely,
  These lovely things beyond our own good will.

And then one said: " Tortesa, here thou sleepest,
  Arise to-night, and watch and hold thy Peace,
And see who cometh when the hour is deepest."
  Tortesa watched—the still stars of Venice,

And saw the master's work—a head of Venus,
  Not half complete, when left the night before—
His trust was deep as sweet wells in Salinas,
  His heart struck like a dipped gondola oar.

Murillo, seeing at the morn 'twas added
  To things made perfect, said, "I charge you all,
Which one will own to this ?" Then some evaded,
  And some denied, on some did silence fall.

Till, lo! the silent slave, sternly commanded,
  Knelt down, confessing with a bended face,
"I heard thee at closed doors, holding, faint handed,
  My heart near where thy words had pleasant ways."

" Ah! didst thou?" said Murillo.   Ask some favor,
    While holding thee to heart, I love and hold;
Where utmost is my hope, thy least endeavor
    Falleth, like Indus waters, over gold."

Tortesa, looking up, half doubting, trembled,
    But finding courage, said the words that live,
Long understood, where'er, wherein dissembled,
    "My father's liberty, oh, Master, give !"

'Unequaled they engage in the battle,
The foreigners and the gael of Tara;
Fine linen shirts on the race of Conn,
And the strangers one mass of iron."
—*Gilbride McNamee, A. D. 1260.*

"If I were an Irishman, I would be a rebel "
—*Sir John Moore,*

THE season was middle May, and then,
By the rocks of the Southwest Sea,
Strong hope grew faint in the hearts of men,
When the French fleet bore away.
But far, where the fir bell hung,
With its creamy cup of dew,
And the lambs' white feet, the meads among,
Bent the grass, the sweet winds blew.

But the dusky glens with their stately heights,
And the Wicklow lakes at rest,
Now breathe no sign of the hearthside blights,
No sign of the hero's breast,

That stained with radiant tide,
  The streams of his mountain home,
Till its life throb seaward billows ride,
  And its banners, worldward roam.

The desolate fields where the reapers stood,
  And the curragh's* meads were broad,
And the wild steep coast of the spray and flood,
  Knew the steps of men outlawed.
And the Hill of Tara shone
  Where the dead so long had lain,
With its beacon fires as in days long gone,
  For a thousand years were vain.

A thousand years were vain to rend,
  Those long tried homes apart,
And again the pike and the bugle send
  A thrill to the peasant heart.
And the stars, like the gold of cloth,
  For tent, by fern and fell,
Made a canopy for the low sworn oath,
  Ere gathered the trumpet's swell.

Then the island days to a stillness came,
  Dismay, but it was not pale,
Heard the yearling babe coo its father's name
  At the door,—heard the wife's last wail:
But his heart was girded strong,
  And his arm of restless might,
Had less of a buckler than its wrong,
  Of a shield, than its native right.

---

*The "curragh" is an extensive rolling plain reaching five miles either way, situated in the county Kildare, Ireland, and invested with much of legendary and historic interest.

Rathfarnham's* flower leaves dense and green
  Were softly bright at morn,
Ere night its bravest dead had been
  Covered by bush and thorn.
And forts that dared success
  In flames and mighty wrath,
Wavered not, till winds grew less
  O'er ashes in their path.

The trees stark branches, gnarled and old,
  Fade slowly, yet to tell
The victim's story, dread and cold,
  Of midnight's tortured wail;
Where anguish, death and jeers,
  With wasting trial failed,
Their ends, from men whose record bears,
  No suffering trust that quailed.

Though riot's toil came close beside
  The tillers' vine hung door,
Where mothers moaned their last, and died,
  Till men were maddened more.
Oh! desperate wild woes,
  Unserried, and apart,
How countless were your grievous throes,
  From casement, street and mart.

---

*In a statement of the insurrection of 1798. D'Arcy McGee
says: "The first intelligence of the rebellion was received in
Dublin on the morning of the 24th of May. At Rathfarnham,
within three miles of the city, 500 insurgents attacked Lord
Ely's yeomanry corps."—*History of Ireland.*

Where Cloghs* sweet village, slopes away,
　　The narrow pass beyond
Grew denser—and its dusk of day,
　　So hushed—grew voiceful toned.
That silent thicket waged,
　　Its bitter blood to lees,
As though the stern dread tempest raged,
　　The cauldron of the seas.

Swift as the loud winged thunder beat,
　　That battle to its height,
There was many a courser's flying feet,
　　And many a man's first fight,
And many a fair head bowed,
　　The silent bier to stain,
The "Kune"† lament of anguish loud,
　　Rose mid the hills refrain.

But cruel, trampling multitudes,
　　That came—those tyrant foes,
To chain those misty mountain floods,
　　Chain'd not such men as those.

---

*Pronounced Clo; at that place, the road descending from the
level arable land, dips suddenly into a narrow and winding
pass. The sides of the pass were lined with a brushy shrubbery, and the roadway at the botom emb nked with ditch and
dyke. On came the confident Walpole, never dreaming that
these silent thickets were so soon to re-echo the cries of the
onslaug. t. * * * Out from the shrubbery rushed the pike-
men clearing ditch and dyke at a bound. Dragoons and fenci-
bles went down like grass before the scythe of the mower; the
three guns were captured, and turned on the flying survivors.
The regimental flags were taken with all the other spoils pe -
taining to such a retreat. It was in truth an immense victory
for a mob of peasants marshalled by men who that day saw
their first or at most their second action.—*See History of Ireland.*

†A thrilling wail over the dead, peculiar to the Irish. Its
weird and haunting cadence recurs to the writer's memory
who heart it many a time in childhood during the Yellow
Fever epidemics at New Orleans.

For many a forest shade,
  And many a rustling stream,
Know where their exiled graves are made,
  Or where their new homes gleam.

As where the rose of Texas blows
  When the soft sun's askance,
To gather new o'er covered brows,
  Left sleeping there by chance,
Whose gaze of sunny blue,
  Beneath sad Erin's skies,
Too proudly browed—too vainly knew,
  Glad hopes's lost destinies.

And when war's banners proudest stream,
  Across *some* battle sky,
Such loyal glance so true doth seem,
  Its patriot's victory.
Although no flowered sword,
  For them.   No trophied urn,
A soldier's grave upon the sward,
  This only—restful bourne.

Lo, as the cross of Constantine,
  Hung dim in rosy clouds,
Thy thousand graves are softly green.
  O'er France's martial shrouds,
With *Harp* and *Lily* rest,
  Prophetic and entwined,
With records faithful to each test,
  And sacred memory shrined.

JOSEPHINE AT MALMAISON.

[The feelings with which Josephine took up her residence at Malmaison amidst the scenes so dear to her may be conceived: but true to the wishes of the Emperor and to the dictates of her own elevated mind she bore up under her trying situation with exemplary dignity. During many hours of the day she shut herself up alone in Napoleon's cabinet, that chamber which she continued to hold so sacred that scarcely any one but herself ever entered it. She would not suffer anything to be moved since Napoleon had occupied it. She would herself wipe away the dust, fearing that other hands might disturb what he had touched. The volume which he had been reading when last there, lay on the table open at the page at which he had last looked, everything seemed as if he were about to enter. * * * * * * * * She would remain for the length of the day alone in the chamber by the large desk conta'ning Napoleon's letters, one of which she was observed to read over and over again and then place in her bosom. It was written from Brienne. A passage in it ran thus: "On revisiting this spot where I passed my youthful days, and contrasting the peaceful condition I then enjoyed with the state of terror and agitation to which my mind is now a prey, often have I addressed myself in these words: 'I have sought death in numberless engagements—I can no longer dread its approach. I could now hail it as a boon. Nevertheless I would wish to see Josephine once more. Adieu, my dear Josephine; never dismiss from your recollection one who has never forgotten you—never will forget you.'"]

H! God, in places olden,
    On plains by hill and shore,
  Wherein the stories folden,
      Seem always, as before,
If Hope, and Faith, and waiting,
Were here to find a greeting,
And my heart's wildest beating—
    Ah!—doubled o'er and o'er.--

See, Lord, Thy ways in fanes
Barred up by custom's chains:
No open port remains
    Where e'er man's foot is found.
But Love's thy spirit's light,
And Life thy mortal blight,
The cloven foot in sight
    One side, with spear wound.

What then!—if the mere seeming,
    Of glance, and lip, and cheek,
A moment o'er me beaming;—
    A sigh, that could not speak,
Oh! God, through thy hands' wringing;
The wild bird hath its singing,
And glad life hath its flinging,
    To where new pulses break,

The very bees have voices,
Unmated blooms have choices,
And streams have anthem noises,
    Yet each knows not the other.
The language hath no signing
By which each can, combining,
Mark where each may, defining
    Call separate need, a brother.

Though no word may be said,
The Shepherd's Star o'erhead
Shines where the dumb are fed,
    Each side a helpless God;
Or at some time before
The waters hushed their roar
And parted shore and shore,
    Each side a Prophet's rod.

O! God, whose ways are changing,
 Even when maples turn,
To where red gold is ranging
 Along the leaves that burn.
"Thou Knowest," and "Thou Knowest,"
And at the last thou showest,
Always so sure, though slowest,
 However long men mourn.

Ah, selfish I, oh Lord!
To pity or call hard
One life without reward,
 Forgetful of Thee—all;
Where streams fall into valleys
To fresh the lily's chalice,
From whence the honey palace
 Rears arch and entresol.

Whereby the flower was growing,
 And shadows fell from trees,
Where wheat will soon be mowing,
 Upon the harvest leas,
Far, far, from where you're dwelling,
Where sunset hills are swelling,
And spring-tide streams are welling,
 I thought such thoughts as these:

So each one's story told
In shimmering shade and gold,
Along where time is scrolled,
 Seemed separate phase apart:
Yet, lo! see how they bend,
Beginning unto end,
So doth thy presence blend,
 Between us, heart and heart.

CARLISLE CASTLE.

[The ancient Castle of Carlisle has succumbed to the march
of utilitarianism. "The people" turned it into a barracks or
factory in 1861 Carlisle was an Augustine priory of monks
and a nunnery, founded in the year 686 It was destroyed in
the Spanish wars, but was rebuilt by William Rufus and Walter, a Norman priest.]

SILENCE had mantl'd for long years thy towers,
Hallowed the mem'ry of departed hours,
With joyousness of steps that went in youth
Glad with the trustfulness of hope and truth,
And firmly girded sword and buckler on,
Pledged for the land the Saracens had won.

Thy lofty arches then re-echoed grand
To solemn music of the choral band,
And softly lighted aisles, filled with profound,
Sweet gentleness of voice; the holy sound
Of nun's most tender prayer and whispered vow,
Those that have sanctified—where are they now?

Some in the quiet chancel still are sleeping,
Where late the tangled ivy low was creeping,
And some in Eastern wilds, where tropic blooms
Of Oleander shade earth's unmarked tombs
With but a flower's soft lustre, void of sign,
That on a pompous slab might mark the line
Of proud ancestral rest, whose sacred fame
Glowed in the lighted crypt's fine chiselled name
Enshrin'd within thee, o'er the distant seas,
Full of the chorus of the centuries.

So sinks thy glory now, before the hand
Of innovation stalking o'er the land.
Even thee it will not spare, oh ancient pile!
For charm of modern art may now beguile,
Clasp of the clinging plant from lintel's edge
Cast where the rip'ling moat's soft swaying sedge
Had glinted in the breaths of tender hours,
And radiance of sun mornings and soft show'rs,
And glow of summer moons above hill brows,
Silv'ry, a mantle on thy ruin throws,
Which, reverential, clothes with tender light
The time-wreck'd splendor of thy silent light.

Now may the revel hold where censor swung,
And where the dim-stain'd windows nightly flung
Weird gleams of mosaic on each pillared crown;
Whose sculptur'd beauty mocked gloom's chasten'd
        frown,
Half veiled from stern decay the frescoed wall,
By stems long matted, clung a rigid pall,
Not since disturbed till now, when crash of doom
May "renovate" and desecrate thy gloom.

DEAD IN THE STEERAGE.

Seven years old, and the delicate rays
  Of shaded Italian skies,
Faded then out from a dear smiling place,—
  Her childish, beautiful eyes.

She was but poor, with the foreign speech
  Of her parents' kindred land,—
Strangers, and sorrowful, standing each,
  Just holding a small dead hand.

Tossed amber rings, where the fever fed,
  Lay out on the canvas strip;
Not all the noise on the deck overhead,
  Brought again the moan to her lip.

The engine clanked—they were going slow—
  The waters grew shallow and green;
They made her a grave, when the ship "lay to,"
  In the Mexican hills between.

Her coffin was boards of the roughest pine,
   Unflowered, untinted of hue,
But over and under they did entwine
   A flag of the starry blue.

Into the long-boat lowered it, then,
   The plash of the oars dipped low,
Bearing it over the soft waves, when
   The sun was brightest at glow.—

When the sun was brightest, at summer glow,
   That never would set for her,
The shoal was broad, like a glad young brow,
   And the bay-washed shells astir.

Like pulses of some child-heart at play
   With the tides and throbs of life,
There's where they made her a grave that day,
   Far, far from the days of strife.

LINES

WRITTEN IN HONOR OF THE OPENING OF THE NEW HALL
ON THE THIRTEENTH ANNUAL COMMENCEMENT OF THE
SANTA CLARA COLLEGE—INSCRIBED TO C. F. WIL-
COX, J. T. MALONE & MARTIN J. C. MURPHY.

———

" Thee, father!" first they sung; "Omnipotent,
Immutable, immortal, infinite;
Eternal king, the author of all being !
Fountain of light, Thyself invisible
Amidst the glorious brightness where Thou sitt'st,
Throned inaccessible, but when thou shad'st
The full blaze of Thy beams, and through a cloud
Drawn round about Thee, like a radiant shrine,
Dark with excessive bright, Thy skirts appear,
Yet dazzle Heaven, the brightest seraphim
Approach not, but with both wings veil their eyes."
                                        —*Milton*.

THE delicate rim of a gilded arch
   Loomed high, to the roofed concave,
   O'er a scene of the amber sun aslant
    On a soft Italian wave.

The painted scene of a Venice Sea,
   Hung rich; and softly dim,
Where the hall was full of the melody
   Of a noble, march-like hymn.

And meet was the offering's shrine that hour
   For the future's memory,
That will go back with a vivid power,
   Ah! more than hauntingly.

For the rose-crowned feet there stood at first,
  While the young heart's flush rose high,
To the loud acclaim of joy's new burst,
  Over cheek, and lip, and eye.

Oh, may their noontide warmth be strong,
  As now their morning light,
And all fruition's charm be wrung
  From proud ambition's height.

No longer pale with student thought,
  The broad young brow that bends
O'er fiery altars, soul-enwrought,
  Where step of science tends.

Where all transfigured,* then as deemed,
  Some mount of knoweledge gained,
The calm, majestic face had seemed
  No longer anxious, pained.

But triumph luminous, in eyes
  Of manly, deep repose:
Stars hold in keeping mysteries,
  Whose keys to them unclose.

An Ocean shadows in his caves
  The colors of soft seas,
But gives their living light from waves
  To soulful eyes like these.

— —

* Suggestive of this idea was the face of the student, *illumined*
on the mount of scientific knowledge; purely pale, sometimes,
in the silver radiance, and anon flushed with the glory of a
thousand scintillations and beautiful colored flames, of violet,
crimson and amber, as the chemical and electrical processes
underwent successive illustrations, till the beholder involun-
tarily exclaimed, gazing at the earnest delineator, "Transfigured on the mount."

How eloquent and bright he came,
   Whose words of feeling fell
Till classic grew our Webster's name,
   Enthroned upon their swell.

As the pure crest upon a tide,
   In tones full organ-grand,
With heartful voice, and theme allied,
   Was step, and brow, and hand.

Long had the slumbrous ages blew,
   Their dust o'er Ægean seas,
But thou an urn hast lighted new,
   To dead Demosthenes.

And not forgotten in the might
   Of all our patriot pride,
Another came to tell the blight
   Of blessings thus denied.

As sorrow's fervor, low and strong,
   And tremulously deep,
Waked from its restless tale of wrong
   The dust of Curran's sleep.

Till all, as many an exiled heart
   Remembered to have seen,
Where distant far, leaning, apart,
   His grave sweet grasses lean.

The hall is hushed; as though he speaks,
   The lustre burneth low;
We hear the mother's heart that breaks—
   The Irish cabin's woe.

Land unredeemed! wait still thine hour,
  For surely it will come;
For thee a voice o'er wrongs that low'r,
  Stirs a new temple's dome.

Be true, be great, be nobly best,
  Though on some hours should fall
From margins of earth's wide unrest,
  The spirit's fainting thrall.

Think of this hour, its arch of light,
  Its flower-entwined feet,
Resolving that life's circuit bright,
  Shall its renewal meet.

COMMUNINGS IN OLD PLACES.

"The shadowy ghosts of our departed years
Will rise commingled with the scenes and thoughts,
And fairy palaces which Fancy built
Upon the airy heights, and changing sands
Of that wild isthmus which alone connects
The past and future—two eternities."
                              —*Bigney's Poems.*

I PASS with a slower step than of yore
  Thy crumbling ruin—my old home door !
    Where the vine-covered mould is greeting
My weary steps, as it erst was wont,
And the violets—each holds its little fount,
  With its drop of dew soft setting.

Let me here for a while call thee back, brown eyes,
And question thee tenderly, for the replies
  Of all that thy thoughts are knowing—
Since joyously bounding over the fern,
Of hour and flow'rs that will never return
  To where thee, and the buds, were growing.

But what is it, shimmering over thee, plays ?
Not the violet's dew, with its scintling rays—
  Not the mists that float in the morning,
As over the golden meadows you look,
Towards the sloping edge of the reeded brook,
  Where the rising sun was burning.

And you played with the wands of yellow cane,
Till the ripples broke in a sweet refrain—
    They were hollow, so like a flute—
But why do you turn from my words away,
Did ever a note from among them stray
    To your heart—and then, was mute ?

See, here are the buds, all lilac and white,
That fell down from the China-boughs at night,
    Hark! the morning's seventh bell,
When the carrolling bird on the branch outside
Trilled sweet his melody far and wide—
    A song with a symbol swell.

There the little church, where the censers burn,
Though their light to thee may never return,
    From under the drooping moss.
Over two small hands there clasped in awe,
You thoughtfully drooped ere you learned to know
    That life had its emblem cross.

Shall I wait, brown eyes, though never a sign,
As you absently gaze where the woods of pine
    Loom over the flowing river—
Till the stately moon, from the clouds unrolled,
Seems as a brow, between hands as cold,
    Over lids, that only quiver.

LINES WRITTEN FOR AN ALBUM.

AFFECTIONATELY INSCRIBED TO MISS MARY KELLY.

* The Lord showed him a tree, which, when he had cast into the waters, the waters were made sweet."—*Exodus, Chapter XV.*
"Till the day break and the shadows retire, return."—*Canticle of Canticles.*

WHERE was a place of waters flowing dull,
    Where Summer died, and murmurs of regret
    Mingled with swaying reed and rocky fret;
The weary prophet trembled in his soul
    When they said unto him, "What shall we drink?"

"Lo! this is Mara," said he unto them;
    The camps of rock and all the torrent's bed
    Heard it forever named as he had said
"Bitter," because they sorrowed blaming him—
    He raised a stricken tree and did not shrink.

Behold the flower and the branch, and hold
    The cups of grief, long empty, unto faith,
    Since on the faces of the waves of death
I cast this as the Lord His wish hath told.
    Thereafter found they strangely it was sweet.

So mayst thou find it, O thou lip of Rose!
    Some leaflet floating from the Syrian breeze
    Of God's great gift to sweeten life with Peace.
Low hangs the middle arch of his repose
    Close to the pattering of thy faithful feet!

COLUMBUS.

[The six following poems were published in the " Era " and the old " True Delta," of New Orleans, La.]

HY pale hands were lifted in prayer
While thy bark on the billow was tossed,
And the angry wave,
A requiem gave
To the men's' buoyant hopes;—that were lost.

The morning light softly came,
And there floated a dark face by;
No vesture or sign,
Of his name or clime,
There came to thine asking eye.

How eager, the spell that lay
On thy parted, quivering lip;
Lifting the head
Of the sea-born dead,
So dark with the water's drip.

What gems of knowledge lay hid
In the gleam of the still cold eye,
As thou gavest again
To the trackless main
Thy pearl, for its treasury.

Then the reeds and wild lilies came
Bright from the unknown shore,
Greeting thy feet
With their fragrance sweet
Strewing thy pathway o'er.

A gleam—in the starless gloom—
Fitful, and lurid, and bright
 It arose to the eye,
 With a sweet mystery,
That fled with the morning's light.

Did not thy great soul feel
A joy in the trackless wild,—
 In the birds' song bowers,
 And sweet wild flowers,
And the homage of Nature's child.

Calling thee thy *true* name,
A messenger sent from on high;
 Regarding thy brow
 With trembling awe,
And the wonderful wings, that could fly.

But thy feet, whom the lilies had kissed,
Dragged to the wearying chain,*
 And thy lone coffin lid,
 Their dark shame hid,
From the eyes of the sons of Spain.

---

*His success and the great mark of favor shown him by his sovereign did not fail to excite envy and jealousy against him in the Court of Spain. In consequence of various false and groundless charges, he was deprived of the government of Hispaniola and sent home in chains. The captain of the vessel in which he returned, through respect to his illustrious captive, offered to release him from his fetters. To whom Columbus replied: "No; I wear these chains in consequence of an order from their majesties, the rulers of Spain. They will find me as obedient in this as in every other injunction. By their command I have been confined and their command alone shall set me at liberty " On his return to Spain in chains the voice of indignation was heard from men of every rank, even Ferdinand seemed to feel the blush of shame. Columbus never forgot this unjust treatment during the remainder of his life. He carried about with him the fetters in which he had been bound and gave orders that they should be buried with him in his grave.—[*M. J. Kerney's Compendium of History.*]

MOTHER.

WE parted, dear mother; and thy gentle eye,
    Looked again, and again, as if fond memory,
      Should cherish the picture forever:
And kissing me tenderly on the still lip,
The last honey dew of the earth might sip,
  I stood looking adown life's river.

And wavelet on wavelet went hurrying on,
Bearing away thy last loved tone,
  Far from thy lonely child,
And flowers there grew by the river's side,
Whose sweetness lay round me far and wide,
  But yet with a waywardness wild.

I sighed for the flowers that floated away,
And looked for their sweetness each sunny day,
  In those that grew by the river,
But the wavelets still went hurrying on,
Saying, child, dost thou expect under the sun
  To find them replaced ever?

MUSIC.

WHAT spell of memory in thy softness lingers,
Touching our hearts as with fairy fingers,
Dripping with tears,
Dimming the joyous eyes, and the "voices gone,"
That come to us in thy silvery tone,
From the vanished years?

Perchance the lovely lips are white, and cold,
Who called thine Eden notes in days of old,
From dreamy rest,
With wandering thought, and half suppressed sigh,
We hear again, the soothing lullaby,
Upon a mother's breast;

Or thou may'st be the mystic song whose tone,
Wafted away, the peace of our heart's home,
Beyond recall;
Coming again, like flowers to the dead,
Making a chaplet for the weary head,
Strewing a pall.

Perchance around some stranger's glowing hearth,
We felt thy sweetness in its joy and mirth,
A welcome share;
May no reproach in thy softness linger,
Touching our hearts as with fairy finger,
Asking a tear.

TWILIGHT REST.

 GORGEOUS gloom lies in the shadow of the
robe of night,
I stand alone beneath the wandering moon's
pale light
And now, anon, 'tis hid beneath a cloud from sight.

The weary cares that haunt with day the tired heart,
Forget their snares and take away their poisoned dart,
That with our fears and hopes had played in cruel sport.

And now the mind to beauteous places, rare and wild,
Flies like the wind, or like the feet of some joyous
child,
Who treasures find where e'er the God of nature
smiled.

Gathering flowers in the soft gloom of green hedge
ways
To cheer the hours, the toil, and dust, of after days,
The twilight pours these as the soft wind plays.

From out the vases and all the beauteous urns,
The lovely places where e'er our memory turns,
They leave their traces, and with incense burns.

THE BLACK HOLE OF CALCUTTA.

THE nabob to Fort William came,—
    Meer Jaffier's haughty Lord,
    And wondered whether sword or flame,
Should fate his fiat's word;

And said with angered loud reproach,
    Why did'st thou dare defend,
Against the ruler of Bengal,
    Before whom all should bend?

The ships went down to Govinepore,
    That could have saved you all,
But on a soldier's word of truth,
    No harm shall you befall.

The English leader, to his men,
    Went back with this glad cheer;
But found the galleries guarded in—
    The quarters all on fire.

And now a dungeon must be found,
  To garrison the men,
The eighteen feet of square "Black hole"—
  A breathless *iron* den.

Behind the close veranda barred,
  One hundred and one-half,
They enter—and each murmured word
  Cut down with scoff and laugh.

Meer Jaffier to his sleep has gone
  And must not be disturbed,
The Jemandars* walk up and down,
  And vainly are implored.

But one who on his face did bear
  The kindest look of all
To pleading cries and looks came near
  For promised rupees' call.

"Must all my men, this horrid night,
  Die at each other's feet,
Poor Holwell said, with eyes of light
  And bitter words unmeet:

"One thousand rupees I will give
  For water, light or air,
They're dying fast, in twos and threes"—
  Ah! incoherent prayer.

---

* Guards.

No change of posture, or relief,
  Till the eleventh hour,
Some skins of water handed through
  Were all th' assuaging power.

And these in struggling hands did make
  But greater the distress,
In curses loud and blasphemies,
  And dying prayerfulness.

The night passed on,—Meer Jaffier slept
  Where none would dare intrude,
And those whom that vigil kept
  But twenty—kept it good.

WELCOME TO THE NORMAL SCHOOL.

THE amber disk of the April moon
  Lights up all the splendid inland lea,
  Like the Champac's lustrous Indian bloom,
Where the Ganges flow to the gates of the sea.

The poplars gleam with their dusky shafts
  Against the opaque of twilight skies;
The silent bird, with a dew damp'd wing,
  More swiftly home to its mate now flies.

The leaves are new on the last year's branch,
  That blows in the warmth of hearth-sides near
The pear-blooms know that their soft flung white,
  For the fruit's sweet sake will soon be sere.

This is the vale by the peaceful sea,
  This is a new world's ambient zone:
The rocks sing the age's minstrelsy,
  Where the tender waves have an organ's tone.

For they know this, more than the cities east,
  Where turret, and palace, and ruin lie,—
The Alhambra's arch, and the jungle's beast,
  The accacia's bloom in the desert's sigh.

Oh! sorrowful, dim old lands of graves;
  Turret and spire, and dome of old;
Dungeons that moan by Venetian waves,
  Let your memories die with their stories told.

Let the loom be still, and the pale hands reach,
　　Aye, children's hands, so thin and small;
See! the bright shells lie on the lonely beach
　　And the woodland flow.rs of springtime call.

Let the smoke roll off from the factory's roof:
　　There the night stays long through the cheerless
　　　　dawn,
Let the weary eyes that gaze on the woof,
　　Come here where the wheat flow'rs bend on the lawn.

And where mists that hung from the Delphic shrine,
　　Bend over the silver hills at n orn,
Where the purple glows of the unpressed vine,
　　Are waiting for nectar gods unborn,—

And the broad facade of a temple's power,
　　Will soon arise where the mountains shine,
Thrice welcome again be the new born hour,
　　Green be the crowns of the laurelled Nine.

The lily shall gleam like a lamp in shade
　　Of the maiden's hair when the groves are broad,
Where a sunbeam wreathing the student's head,
　　Will seem as a stray sweet smile of God.

The eagle shall sit on its highest cone,
　　And the silver feet on the heights shall be,
And the sacred dust of the "Pantheon,"
　　Shall arise from the tombs of memory.
San Jose, Cala.

THE FUNERAL OF ALBERT SIDNEY JOHNSON.

HE fell!—and they cried, "bring us home our
  dead,
  We'll bury him here, where the prairies' spread,
And the Gulf waves beat on our Southern shore;
He will hear them not, when he comes, once more,
  Our Albert Sidney Johnson.
When he went, how the flush of hope beat high
On the brows of the "Rangers" standing nigh,
And the champion steeds of the Texas plain,
For his voice was that, to their bridle rein,
  That the air 's to the Persian monsoon.

 * * * * * * * * *

They bore him then o'er the crash of wheels,
No sound of their sorrow the hero feels,
While many are come that are sad and fair,
With the flower and star for his bloody bier,
  And weeping they laid them down,
And the crescent shone with a wreathing grace
Around *that star* on his covered face,
No sound, but of sobs, and a parting look,
And the forest night where the damp winds shook
  As the train went rumbling on.

Down to the feet of of the mourning sea,
Where the sands made the only melody,
No band, or bell, was played or tolled,
But the hero cared not,—hate fell cold
    On the heart of him who slept,
Where the church was closed, by the mandate given
While he lay on the wharf under night—and heaven.
Fair friend, and *slave*, with uncovered head—
Gazed alike, on the face of the dead,
    And alike in silence wept.

So the vigil held, till the chastened cloud
For the shame of man hid its head and bowed,
And thousands came when the moon was high
And bore the cortege sadly by,
    For his home was nearing then,
As the prairie flowers, that now grow o'er him,
Were the white maned steeds that walked before him,
Proud stepped, and slow; and the mourners said,
Let a stately place for his couch be made,
    Houston will have a fane.

So they laid him out in a proud old hall,
Where the floor's edge kissed the sacred pall,
And thousands came to that hallowed room,
Till the day went down to the night of gloom,
    For his land did honor him,
And when to the bannered march's swell
They bore him out with a lingering knell,
Thousands there from the hallowed room
Went out that day to the night of gloom,
    For the sun in the west was dim.

ALL the summer's golden June,
   The August and September time
   The river's mild, deep undertone,
The landed steamer's morning chime,
I knew, and knowing day by day,
   One year of years, now seventeen,—
And then my joy was glad and mute
Then came your babyhood's salute,
   The little mouth of my delight,
Is coaxing up its first mustache,
   And tiny brows are brows of might
Where manhoods years may feel and flash,
The grace of time—the world's worth,
May hail them as new thrones of earth,
But know, erewhile, ambition feels
The rough roads of the chariot wheels;
Soft awfulness of grief is made
Sometimes of brows with glory bayed,
Ah; nameless chronicles are naught,
If Life with Love and Peace be fraught,

The golden helm is one true hand
Whose warmth is not a battle brand.
And like pure shafts of Orient towers,
The chastened thoughts of youthful hours
A stronger sun more splendid falls,
On their full beauty's coronals,
  Be strong like ships that fearless go,
Be cautious like still leaves at night,
  Be prayerful; so thy star shall glow,
By wave and shore in pathless light.

"FOUND DEAD."

" A grave for the stranger."—*New Orleans paper*.

PALE is thy cheek,—and hid the frozen tear
    Beneath the brown lash in whose gentle gleam
Dwelt love for some one whose unconscious
    prayer
May seek it henceforth on the earth in vain.

Now we may take thee by the cold, cold hand
    That is no more for sympathy extended,
Perhaps a stranger in a stranger land,
    With not a kindred brow above thee bended.

Silence is on thy lip;—no word or name,
    By which to know thee, or thy sad, sad tale,
Thy proud heart lonely in its grief, and shame,
    Breathed sorrow only to the winter's wail.

Where may thy home be, or thy gentle mother,
    'Tis well she sees thee not, if such thou hast,
We give thee to the quiet earth, our brother;
    Alas! we give thee but a grave at last.

GARDEN WALKS AT NOTRE DAME.

INSCRIBED TO A——I F—T—D.

OW chanced it that together we should so
   Have ever met? She of the presence bright,
   With cloth of white bound up about her brow,
And tender eyelids over azure light—
As mild as Heaven, or as the violets sweet,
That fringed the garden path down at her feet.

Sometimes she stopped at white sprays near her hand,
   Where bees with plumy wings went forth and back,
To some orchestral lily, whose sweet band,
   Swung low the music censor for her sake.
I thought how like they were to messengers,
Out from and to her heart all its life hours.

She was the spirit that they typified,
   In flow'ring time of stem and coronal,
Whose music-pulses to her heart replied,
   As mem'ries sweet and bright she did recall,
With smile and gesture and soft step held still,
And soul aglow with nature's holy thrill.

The wall was mossy on its margin near,
    Where just before some distant woodland singer
Had flown, and left his echo matin pray'r,
    Just where he knew her steps would come and linger,
With colors of glad blossoms, finger-twined,
The while one thought how seemed they to her mind.

"Why not love God," she said; "it is but right
    That he who made our thoughts should have their
        best,"
And here she put a tender spray of white
    Amongst the violets in their emerald nest;
Though all unconscious, like a lyre in tune,
Her fingers with her thoughts held sweet commune.

The time will come, I know, when even this
    Will only have been in the drifts of years;
But let me keep its calm remembrances—
    A dew of Hermon amongst many tears.
A soft " thou knowest " from some quiet deep,
That answers unto all its vigils keep.

FLOWERS GATHERED ON THE WAY HOME.

FLOWERS gathered lonely where—
  When the day's long labor's done—
  Thoughts come like a worldless pray'r
Of some darling at home.

These are flowers, and not words,
  With a speech of tongue—the token
Is that music on whose chords
  Speech is felt, but is not spoken.

Tints of evening, ambe clouds,
  With the purple cascandes near them;
Birds all flying home in crowds,
  Singing, though but few may hear them.

They mean this, and something more,
  Shells upon the ocean beaches,
Scattered 'long the sounding shore,
  Out of breaker's cruel reaches.

They mean hands earth cannot grasp,
  Spirit hands high faith upholding,
White palms for stronger ones to clasp,
  Like petals honeyed sweets enfolding.

"A HOME OF LANG SYNE."

" Shall auld acquaintance be forgot."

MY father planted the China trees,
   That cover its old roof o'er,
     And brother and sister played in the breeze—
That wandered by its door.

But some are gone far over the seas,
   And some will play no more:
They're laving their woe tired feet in the waves,
   That wash Eternity's shore.

Well I remember the creeping vines,
   With their blossoms purpling through,
And the roses that laughed to the summer winds,
   And the violets sweet that grew.

And the little glass door, with its clear white panes
   That charmed the sunlight through
On the pine floor in shadowy stains,
   With many a varying hue.

And the dim old loft with its books "galore,"
   That many an hour beguiled,
With their pictures of grim old kings of yore,
   And many a legend wild.

And then the charms of the other old loft,
    All sweet, with its new mown hay,
That tampted my wandering feet so oft,
    To find where the hens would lay.

And the wild, wild songs we used to sing,
    Coming from school in the field;
Oh, the joy that in their tones did ring,
    No music on earth will yield.

And the old oak trees that grew in a clump,
    That we were afraid to pass;
Where the ghost who reigned might be only a stump,
    And the sounds the waving of grass.

And don't you remember, dear S—ve, the night
    That we had to pass it by,
All the prayers we said, and the fright,
    We suffered, you and I,—

And how closer together we pressed,
    And walked as fast as we could,
And how happy we were, and blessed,
    When we got past the wood ?

How many woods darker and drear,
    We meet in the journey of life,
With no clasping hand to quiet our fear,
    But all alone in the strife.

But we may remember the prayers we said,
    And walk straight on to the right,
Until we come to the edge of the wood,
    And enter Eternity's light.

AT BOULIGNY (now called Jefferson City,) La.

HEN the silent spray of the meadow grass,
  By the wind is bent low on the lea,
  In your path—and the cars so swiftly pass
Pensez a moi, mon cher amie.

When the sun is high at the noon of day,
  And the shadows slant by the wayside tree,
And you say "Sweet, rest by the tired way,"
  Pensez a moi, mon cher amie.

When the hearths of distant homes are bright,
  And you think of the vale by the vesper sea,
One minute, sweet; be it e'er so slight,
  Pensez a moi, mon cher amie.

If you wake when the stars are amethyst,
  And go where their light shines breathlessly,
Oh, then, let it be that I shall be missed.
  Pensez a moi, mon cher amie.

H, Venice! I have seen thee when the light
  O'er thy gondolas gemmed the soft lagoon
With tints magnificently golden bright,
As is the radiance of the sun at noon.

And where, behind the mountains of the Rhine,
  As idly on the Nectar's bank I lay,
I watched the Heidelberg's old towers define
  Themselves in changing hues of dying day.

But here, where no trace on the desert lay,
  Save the dim tracks the wheels can scarcely find,
And the sweet wells which mark the winding way,
  To bless the shepherd's thirst or roving hind.

There night came, and we slept, and were alone,
  And lo! at morn, after our troubled sleep,
All things were new, and while the glad sun shone,
  A lake and landscape spanned the upper deep.

It was a mirage; but it looked so fair,
  That we approached it, and would not believe,
Till arid plains, as lone as hopeless prayer,
  Unmasked the brilliancies that e'er deceive.

We gazed, and wondering saw a river bright,
    Extending far along the still background,
Girt with a distant wood that charmed the sight,
    And park-like made that olden forest's bound.

But soon dividing with a sweet half view,
    A village, just commencing like a hope,
Appeared and passed, and then distinct grew
    The barren plains beneath the fading group.

"*LA PETROLEUSE.*"

WHERE with the passing dread on her,
 And nothing more to gain or lose,
 With revolvers pointed two or more,
You may shoot her now for a Petroleuse.

Twelve months ago, even so late,
 She was a woman good and true,
But how was it all in the siege, her fate
 Grew red with crime and pale with woe.

How was it all, ere grief began
 To turn to shame, her mild cheek blushed
With its changing tears, like Peristan,
 When after the rain its skies are flushed.

They lied; in the crowd where she was hissed,
 She's *not* from the slums of Paris taken,
As the libelers of the Versaillist
 Say of them all, doomed and forsaken.

No! she will not tell her name,
 Nor of her home or husband, nor of more;
How when school was out, her children came
 With happy footsteps to the door.

First, work grew scarce, and her husband, then,
    Ere he shared with her their last poor meal,
Kissed her and bid her good-by, when
    They wanted men in the *Garde Mobile.*

Then the siege came, and the snow and frost,
    And daily where the poor were fed,
She waited, too—not least, not most,—
    And silent and half comforted.

*   *   *   *   *   *   *   *   *

But she fled when the last of her children died,
    The night lamps lit a deserted *porte*
When the voices in the street outside
    Shouted, "*Commune, ou la mort.*"

So there with the last cold dread on her,
    And nothing more to gain or lose,
With revolvers pointed two or more,
    You may shoot her now for a Petroleuse.

"INCLINE UNTO MY AID."—AN ACROSTIC.

" He shall judge among nations; he shall fill ruins; he shall crush the heads in the land of many."—*Psalm* 109.

IVINE thy right is, let it be well done,
And from thy signal name my armor take
Into the light of all the strong things won,
Now wilt thou say to me " sit near my hand,"*
Giving my sad soul peace; for thou can'st make
Even a footstool as it was foretold,
Roused thou he be mine enemy of old;—
Forward a little, from the white robe's band
Is the pressed sandal on his shining neck,
Each, to the fire-kissed lips the low doves speak,
Let this be seen by thee:—"make straight thy word
Dear though its cost,—"The pathway of the Lord."

---

* "Sit thou at my right hand, until I make thy enemies thy footstool."—*Psalm* 109.

ANNIE LEE.

Then Annie, with her brows agains* the wall,
Answered "I cannot look y< u in the face."
"I a^ content" he answered, "to be loved a little after Enoch."
— *Tennyson.*

T is not that I love him best,
　'Tis only that I can't attest
　　Thy love before his throne;
Than pride thy hope was only less,
And that hope filled with tenderness,
　But his heart was my own;

I held it where no human love,
Since or before, dare throb above
　　So wild a misery;
And years have fled with only dreams,
And yet the end so far seems
　In years that are to be.

His soul was just as proud as thine,
But all its right he did resign,
　　Though even death might see;
Upon my heart he laid his hands,
And only mine since understands
　All that the cost might be.

ALTSAY BURN, OR THE RAID OF CILLIE-CHRIST.*

* Christ Church.

I.

WHOSE sides with flowery garlands hung,
 Whose winds with Ossian's harp had had sung,
 Whose dense, dark birch the bottoms line
With purple heath and feathery pine,
Made beautiful,—whose gray rock rose
Against the sunset sky's repose—
The azure, light-incumbent sky,
Reached unto, as by Alps as high,
Where straggling falls the knotty ash
From storm-reft ledges with a crash;
Where footsteps pause to seek return,
This is the gorge of Altsay Burn,
Not all whose beauty here I tell,
But mark this much for what befell:

II.

 Glengarry's chief held Angus dear,
The eldest son, Macdonell's heir,
The foray's leader, when the clan
War'd with Mackenzie, man to man.
Angus was tall and strong, they say,
As Coromandel's lithe Palmae,

And fearless as the stag whose leap
Is sure, or else the death that's deep.

III.

The dews were light on Cillie-Christ,
And Janet Lyle's soft step the least
Of many gentle sounds that made
Her quick and venturous heart afraid.
But there was Angus coming near,
With smiles and thanks that she was here.
She loved the chief, Glengarry's son,
And he loved her—that love was one—
With graves whereon they stood that hour
Of omen, with the moonlit flow'r;
With all things deep and sad, with things
Whose tim'rous promise never brings
The olive from the dove's wet wings.

IV.

Home from the foray's cheered success,
Glengarry's turned, their band not less;
Mckenzie's in the Beauly firth,
Defeated, knew their valor's worth,
But swore with vengeance-bated breath,
To track young Angus to his death;
While homeward did his footsteps turn,
They never came to Altsay Burn.
The hill was steep, th' assassin's hand
Had signal tryst of all his band,
And cutting through the faithful ring,
That round a chief in clamor cling,
With eyes that flamed and cheek that flushed,
They closed and clenched, the deadly grasp,

In silence Angus—Donald's gasp,
Was muttered cursing—and a minute,
Had all the fate of either in it.
Then Angus, with unplaided throat,
Turned faceward, saying, ere 'twas smote,
"There, Donald Lyle, when I am slain,
Tell *her* I would do this again."

v.

That day a lamentation rose,
Glengarry's vales echoed their woes,
And rugged hearts, where grief was hard,
Pledged Clan MacKenzie sure reward.
Gather! Gather! from every hill,
Rung out to Allen MacRaonuill,
The Lord of Lundy, leading them
Across the hills whence late they came,
Well-favored, marching under night
On to the scene of speedy blight.
They reached it when the Sunday sun
With chapel service had begun;
Then lighter grew each footstep's beat,
And whiter grew each cheek's white heat;
The distant twitering of a bird,
Could on the birch's branch be heard—
The sacred walls of Orison
Let no sight seen of anyone,
The sacred sound of prayer within
Made little note of outside din;
Till all surrounded it was held
At door and window sentineled.
And then—the very heart recoils,—
The brands have blazed around their spoils

To seething flames; the claymore's clash
Falls quickly, where the foremost's rash
In efforts to escape despair,
With cursing shriek or pleading pray'r,
The gasping breath no more recalled,
All make the mind shrink back appalled;
And while the victims, tortured, die,
The Pibroch's shrill note heard on high,
With ghastly triumph made each death
A mockery of its mingled breath—
Of child and mother, man and man,
But few were left Mackenzie's clan.

VI.

But in their turn those few soon turned
To mustered strength where vengeance burned;
And tracking dastard steps, took heed
Of twofold slaughter's double deed.
Dividing forces, two and two,
One followed all the southside through,
Whose longest chase was over, when
Macdonell's halted in the glen.
Then both the clans, though fainting, burned
With hot revenge, each deadly turned
Upon the other's rancorous wrath;
Their dead were mingled in their path,
Their mutual fury, strength of arm
And swiftness, kept an even charm.
At length Macdonell's numbers, less,
Were driven in their last distress
To the wild torrent's rugged side,
In tumbled, or fell first, and died.

VII.

Mac Raouuill, strong, athletic frame,
Held longest to his valor's fame,
And having made his flight the best
To where the torrent 'tensely pressed,
A narrow chasm—death to miss,
He meant to leap the dread abyss,
While hot pursued, he took a glance—
The depth, the breadth, the desp'rate chance,
And blind with danger, fierce with hope,
With venture he would dare to cope
Success.   O, heaven! his sure foot
Is safe!   Mackenzie in pursuit,
With less of strength and length of limb,
And less of the wild stag in him,
Leaps after, falling short, the brink
Grown sapling in his grasp must shrink.
Mac Raouuill turns,—the dangling wretch
Looks upward, and his eyes beseech,
Mac Raouuill, coming nearer, took
His dirk, with fiendish smile, and struck
The sapling, saying, "Take that too,
I've given much to-day to you."

AGA MOHAMMED.

[The avarice of this monarch was often the cause of awkward
and ludicrous incidents. The following, related by Frazer,
bears such a striking and amusing comment on many every
day human motives, that we trunspose it.]

AGA Mohammed was great and wise;
A mendicant once prostrated lay
In the path of his train, at the noon of day,
On whom the benevolent cast his eyes.

"Give him an alms," the monarch said;
(And between us here it may just be told
That Aga Mohammed was fond of gold;)
But "God is great," let gifts be spread !

And they were,—for, lo, the courtiers all,
Observing well their gracious king,—
'Twas thus the bulbuls learned to sing—
Gave to the mendicant, great and small.

The pious monarch and all his train
Moved onward through the adoring crowd,
Whose tendered homage'was deep, not loud,
Till the hour of pray'r at eve again.

Then night came over Khorassan's vales;
Baba, and Jaffer, and Houssin Khan
Sat where the fountains rippled and ran,
To fill their chibouks and tell their tales.

But Aga Mohammed was ill at ease,
On piles of cushions although reclined;
His brow was sad, and his temper pined;
In vain his ministers tried to please.

"Oh, Allah! this morning that scoundrel lied
That was prostrate there in the crowded street.
The dog of a Christian! Oh, the cheat!"
With sorest impatience the monarch cried;

"The rogue! he promised to give mine back
Along with half what the others gave.
Haste, Mirza! bring me the arrant knave;
I'll give him the Bosphorus and the sack!"

But in vain were the horsemen ordered out,
The fellow was off full many a mile,
And the courtiers did not dare to smile
At the vain return of each weary scout.

SWINBURNE PLEADING TO SAPPHO.

[The following lines embody the Pythagorean idea, that the soul of Phaon, whom Sappho so hopelessly loved, was born anew into the body of Swinburne, than whose heart no more appropriate and retributive Hell "Circle" could be created. Those familiar with the writings of Swinburne, and the story of Sappho and Phaon, will perceive the suggestiveness.]

"Lucadia's rock still overlooks the wave."—*Byron.*

TIME lingers; anthen s break from sudden wind;
  Leaves from the trees rush like the startled hind,
  And the dim shadows glancing o'er the sea,
Arise, all charged with troubled melody;
Judgments arrayed, impassioned of its theme,
(That I, thy Phaon, should have lived to dream,)
Returned evasive meanings of all time,
Sick—for thy beauty—for thy voice's chime.
More than assuaged for centuries thy part,
Stung with the thorns of roses at thy heart,
As filled with wrath of travil thou wouldst not
Rest like the sea-dirged dead, and be forgot.
Incense of Pyrrho, for the perished lays,
And blooms of night, whose sweets fill scattered ways;
Sparkling of sudden fire with serpent fold,
Wound off, the years and tears, that were untold.

Sleep cometh with her hands closed fast on flowers,
That perish brown, and fall among the hours;
While wafts of gale-blown grief won from the sea,
Brought only sorrow unto me and thee;
But never from the storm that doth arouse,
Gleaned she the riches of red coral boughs,
Or blossom-kisses of thy panting mouth,
Honeyed by dews of the soft balmy South,
With thrills of shame too swiftly drawn away—
Terror that on thy breast my lips did stay;
Surely new vengeance found a beaten path,
With all the subtle tortures that she hath;
Mem'ry and madness, and the thoughts that wring
Thy passionate heart with keenest suffering;
Whispers from lips, that fall on lips too tame
To thrill with passion or to pale with blame,
Story of seasons, long and far apart,
From this day, and the day you felt my heart
Beat at your own too fast to even stay
One little hour of all Life's hours, away,
For sapphire drifts of years, that sad go by,
Shaded with lustre of thy pleading eye,
And veins of amethyst, like flower stems urned
Between thy white neck and my lips, that burned.
Oh, Love, one moment, let it be; I plead,
For all the life of sorrow's piteous need;
See how my mouth thy mouth's sad words repeats;
Feel how my heart thy heart's sad music beats;
Silence the audience of the solitude,
Be soft and tender, for a changed mood,
Fashioned within the raiment of a gloom,
Knowing thee love; as it was said of whom
They nailed beside the road, and then denied;
But knew the God of Gods when He had died.

Full of the pain that never perisheth,
And twined with stray sobs of thy mused breath,
Choosing the stories that all men may read,
And count the measure of a ruined heed.
With my hands bared upon the wild black mane
Of life, the lion of a new born pain;
Seek thee, and find thee not, but find a thing—
A heaviness of tongue, strange songs to sing,
And fiery dreams of joy disquieted,
All sorrowful to know, shame-kissed, and fed,
Telling the color of thy closed eyes,
And clothing with a raiment all thy sighs,
And twining all the shapes of sweet limbs dead,
Into an agony that none would wed;
With low and soft-winged words, lit up again,
By all thy cruel prayers and cruel pain;
Full of the weight of an unlaid repose,
As is the sea that hides thee where it flows.

THE HILLSIDE RIDE.

HE broad Alameda was shady and long,
  By fences and trees, where birds full of song,
  Said, "beautiful morning," as plain as they
    could,
So away we rattled, by villa and wood.
April was near, and her dainty, light feet
Were full ankle deep in the emerald wheat;
By and by deftly she'll take it and fold
Over her instep its bandlets of gold,
Like a Nizam's daughter in rank is she—
A queen of the acres so broad and free.

We left Santa Clara far, far behind;
What cared I for my cheeks growing brown in the wind,
For the scene was sublime, and a trifling veil
Would only have served the fair view to curtail.

Just here I'll remark, in my private confession,
That I passed the next day at my leizure's discretion,
In holding some buttermilk over my nose,
For, (seeing it's you, I don't mind to disclose),
That owing to breezes suburban, and solar,
My nose had a very remarkable color!
However, as taletellers say, "We'll return
To our story." The ride over hillside and fern,

Poor Jenny was dry, when we came to a pool,
She drew in the wheels, and she drank where 'twas cool.
Now, if she were a donkey, instead of a mare,
She'd have done, I've no doubt, just the same thing
    there.

The myrtle and marigold glittered and quivered,
Where shadows of poplar leaves on the sward shivered,
Then, away and away, soon nearer and nearer,
The sky and the flowers grew brighter and clearer,
When they were before us—the hills; O, the hills.
With torrents from mountains, that slumber in rills,
And cañons that cradle the records of time,
On boulders of stone with their mysteries sublime,
And the waters still flow with a sacred sound,
Whose utterance falls on the silence round,
Like the Oracle's power, of Delphic peace,
In the hollows of seas, by the Isles of Greece.

On a laurel browed edge, there we rode at risk,
Near a daring brink; the revolving disk
Of the wheels held Death o'er the beams of a bridge,
Or the turn sf some sudden curve in the ridge.

I thought of my sins, and the dash below,
With next moment the change of a rapturous "Oh!"
As the rocks and the flowers, the surge and the cliff,
Grew brighter, and sweeter, and broader as if
Some world I had left, in some other Life's Death,
Was back there before me upon the spring's breath;
But oh! as one comes to a hearth found cold,
I found myself thinking some thoughts of old.

I pitied the nameless thing growing near by,
With the purple of sunset all over its dye;
And I thought how lonely its seed had been thrown,
Where the wind blew a little of dust on a stone,
And the seedling thought, full of hope, no doubt,
"What a nice high place I shall have to sprout."
So the anxious bloom of a chastened wrath
Grew there, in the wind, on the rock's hard path.
No tender place could I see for its fall,
When its bloom should go back to its life's recall;
There was only the bed of the gulch below,
Where the rocks break up and the west winds blow
From the sea; and the torrents, through crushing
     arcades,
Break out from the gates of the hills, on the glades.
I knew it would perish in falling down,
With its tender leaves and amethyst crown,
So I stretched my hand, and reaching for it,
I said, "I shall take you and call you 'pet!'
I shall save you from loss; I shall put you where
I have other flowers, in a garden fair;"
And kissing my wild thing, so violet-eyed,
For sake of two lips on this life's other side,
That might say, I could hear them, "I see that you do
Unto others, my flower, as is done unto you."

     * From San Jose to Lexington.

LINES.

THINK'ST thou not, my heart was sad, to weeping,
    On seeing thy step once joyous now so slow;
    Ah yes! though under smiles the sorrow keeping,
With all the things that Life may never show.

But now, with after thought and lonely hours,
    And in the quiet stillness of mid-watch,
It will be heard for all its many powers,
    And for the fond love that forgiveth much.

It will be heard for sake of happy years,
    Where clustered vine, and bird, and flower, and bee.
And for the sake of sweet and treasured tears,
    That lie in graves beyond the summer sea.

And for the sake of that sad care o'er shading,
    The brow whose earliest signs my own hath known,
Too well, for smile, or jest, their life evading;
    Giving strange splendor to their weary tone.

But stars shall wane, oh tender brother mine,
  Ere mirthful eyes shall cease to veil the heart,
But in their misty depths, like lees in wine,
  The pain well-mated knows its counterpart.

The songs, whose spirit tone hath vanished long,
  And whose sweet chords are yet called melody,
But not the voids can music fill with song,
  As with dead flowers, the caves of the sad sea.

    ·

IMPROMTU.

A PROPHECY FOR MY FAIR MISS MARY L—HY.

THE day's rose red,—the frontlet's shield,
  Of all the stars in heaven's field,
  And strange, deep, grand blooms of the sea,
  Will yet come very near to thee.

THE TRI-COLOR ON THE SPIRE AT METZ.

[The famous French tri-color is still flying from the spire of the cathedral at Metz. The Prussian authorities have made every effort to have it removed, but without success. They have vainly offered large sums of money to any adventurous person who would climb the steeple and remove it, while their sharpshooters have uselessly fired thousands of shots at it. The people have come to look at the lone flag as a good augury. They say with enthusiasm that the flag of France still floats above them, and when the breeze extends its folds in the direction of the Rhine, they point to it and say to each other in the streets, "Look! we shall have a fine day, the wind comes from France!" There is said to be in all Metz only one man who is both skillful and daring enough to climb the steeple to its entire height. This is he who placed the flag there. He is a poor workman who, during the war, attached the flag to the peak of the spire for five francs; but the patriotic Frenchman has refused the Prussian Governor's offer of 5,000 francs to remove it.—*Exchange.*]

LIKE a life with its heart of rose,
   And the blue of the deep's repose,
     And the wing where a white dove goes
  To the Rhine, if the still winds may,
With an altar for its throne,
  On the spire at Metz alone,
From the rise to the set of sun
  Flies the flag of France to-day.
Look! the people say—and they look,
Not a shot of a thousand struck;
'Twas the silk dews filled and shook
  Its folds, while the night was long.
Now the day will be lifted fine,

For the breeze blows out to the Rhine
From the olive hills and vine—
  From France blows warm and strong.
There is one, one daring hand,
Only one in the whole full land,
Only one firm foot to stand.

  He raised—will he strike it low?
At a call he came from the ranks,
For a meager gift of francs,
And his heart's love for his thanks.

  Is his name Constantine?   No!
And he did not place it higher
Than the cross in the clouds of fire;
Yet the daring hour at the spire

  Of Metz shall a standard be
When the burning Louvre smokes not,
And the barricades, unsought
With the tempters' francs, shall rot,

  While the Seine flows on to the sea.

THE HAUNTS OF THE GREEK BRIGANDS.

IN the Raphini wood, with mist and rain
    The hillside copse, pine-hung, shows darkly near.
  "Night on Pentelicus," and o'er the plain,
    Where deep Cephissian winds the travelers hear,
Not with the Oread music of the past,
But with harsh threats which rose upon the blast.

In the green calms of some long trodden pass,   -
    Some place as far as Deccleia's sea,
Three thousand feet below.   Whose loveliness,
    With Phidian rocks grow hoarse, and mourn for thee,
Cradle of sorrow; unappeased—and wrong,
Now the Albani hath grown fierce and strong.

Strong by the fireless hearth to night's rapine,
    From huts long shelterless, the shepherd goes,
Where silver harness clanks beside each shrine,
    And idle gazers come, and move the rose
From dear Castalie, where sweet fountains fret
Over some scribbled name, or coronet.

Where the bright arbutus alone should be,
    Recorder of sweet tracings, in the glow
Of suns, on slopes that reach Thermopylæ,
    Where the loud organs of the strong waves flow,
With old time music—where the rocks arise,
By Corinth, under glows of South sea skies.

Egean beauty, let thy calmness grieve;
　Let all the prestige of devotion's zeal,
Give to thy burdened claims what may reprieve,
　The sorrow of revenge's vain appeal,
For him,* who died there, whom her laurels crowned—
Let England deem thee more than classic ground.

Mount of Eubea! where their† last look turned,
　Cover thy face from the Delphian vale;
They slept—with hopes beneath thee, dimly urned—
　Thy desolation heard a lingering wail—
In the flute breathings over Platean tombs,
Another tone shall wander where it roams.

. * Byron.
　†The victims of the Greek massacre.

THY LITTLE CHILDREN.

INSCRIBED TO THE LATE MRS. CHAPMAN, DAUGHTER OF
MR. AND MRS. DAN MURPHY.

"Oh! happy! if to them, the one dread hour
Made known its lessons from a brow like thine."
—*Hemans.*

THEY, who will love thee, and cannot remember
    All the full sweetness of thy young life here,
    Ere the last days of heavy-dewed September;—
What lingering signs shall whisper of thee, dear;

Transfixed forever each high thought's pure feeling,
    Thy lit-eyes' splendor, and thy gentle voice,
Soft looks, light footsteps; ah! what charm revealing
    Life's worth shall show them, that one charm that
        was.

Thy tender patience, strong and brave and purest,
    Would break for them, death's fastness with thy
        heart,
But the stern secret that so long endurest
    Once more's a spell;—thy radiant better part.

Near to thee, sleeper; when the Spring returneth,
　With seed flowers on the breeze,—their little feet
Will come and wait, while low, the soft sun burneth
　O'er little lips so long unkissed, and sweet.

Thine, like two soft leaves of a white rose faded,
　Have left their smiles to love's unchanging faith,
Though Nature weeps—what hast *thou* evaded
　Of cares and griefs, on Time's untraversed faith.

Above the lifted mists of shining willows,
　Their childhood's joy-hushed eyes may wond'ring
　　　gaze,
While loving lips may say, "behold the billows,
　Such was the grandeur of thy mother's days.

Bright, deep, and placid, unto love completed—
　Now a sweet slumberer,—one image left,
Tranquilly lovely as her steps retreated,
　Nay! not all bitterly, we weep bereft."

SAN JOSE, October 2d, 1876.

THE TOKEN RING OF ESSEX AND ELIZABETH.

SOME day, beloved;—some other year,
  When scorn is dumb, and anger cold,
  I know just how you'll say: "yes, dear."
I wish I'd been less stern of old,
I know just what your thought will be,
  Finding some page forgotten where,
Your hand will lift it tenderly,
  As though you softly touched my hair.

And you will say: "I gave her this,
  I taught her all its mystic lore,
The perfect great Eternities :
  The meanings of forever more,"
And I shall there in silence sit,
  I shall not answer quickly then,
But soon across this hour shall flit,
  A patient memory of pain.

The sweet tears shall not fall too swift,
  Perhaps forever they'll be dried,
Where midnight aye; nor morn shall light,
  Their seals from graves which flowers half hide,
The plashing gulf with drifting sprays,
  That inland to the blossoms blow,
Shall in their own dear tender ways.
  Leave buds for fingers, and—I'll know.

THE LITTLE BOY THAT DIED AT SEA.

" The angels warbling their celestial psalms,
Hath for thy coronal a golden throng
Of everlasting s'ars "—Tasso.

'TIS fitting that requiems of the deep
   Now hover around thee in thy sleep;
    They murmur for thee, in their own sweet way—
Ripple, and wind-waving wave-crowned spray,
   So like thee, fairest—who passed away.

No flow'r or bird on thy pallet lies;
But only the sunlight on thine eyes;
Not the passionate sobs of the troubled deep,
Shall waken them ever again, to weep,—
   For their holy watch now the angels keep.

For thee is the summer south wind sweet,
Where foam-wreaths break at thy fair young feet
Like pale hands pressed, in their stricken grief
For the lost young life so loved and brief—
   That left not with love a pang's reprief.

Thou'rt gone; but see! how the pearl-clad sky
Proclaims how near is thy home on high,
Where the star-crowned night and the sun-robed day
Hath borne from the earth a new light away—
   With thine angel brow, on their throne to stay.

THE SNOW UPON THE HEIGHTS AT SAN SAN JOSE, CAL.

I LOOKED upon the wintry day;
　　The heavy mist lay still,
　Like a dense curtain stretch'd away
　　Across each rugged hill.
The stream grew to a torrent's roar,
　　Birds flitted near in flights,
And lovely, though like lances were
　　The gleams upon the heights.

The troubled well still murmureth,
　　Its cascade's fervid song;
I think in human words and breath,
　　It means, "so long, so long."—
Some sparkle dark, like steel-clad spears,
　　Some pale,—like flower blights,}
But lovely, through the mist appears
　　The snow upon the heights.

The willlow wands stand naked now
　　Before the silver east,
And sharp from the Sierras blow
　　The winds across the waste—
Like leopards' sides, the heavy foam
　　In flecks of dark and white,
Rolls up amid seas to the home
　　Of snows upon the heights.

SUNSET IN CALIFORNIA.

The sun glared behind with ruddy beam
Before my form was broken; for in me
His rays resistance met. I turned aside
With fear of being left, when I beheld
Only before myself the ground obscured,
When thus my solace turning him around,
Bespake me kindly.   —*Dante.*

I SEE thee, sunset of the distant West,
  In halos and rich shadows unconfined.
  I feel thy spirit thrilling on the wind,
Voices of melody in trembling quest,
Of flute-breathed places in the cascade's breast,
Thou art not e'er o'erworn—thy bannered right
Is always beautiful, forever bright,
Waking high kindred in the soul divine,
Deep answering mysteries all so like to thine,
Not in thy colors or their blending tone,
Or in the light mist o'er their ambience thrown.
Thy realm hath more than these—through rock and
    stream,
Whose liquid passion in dark places gleam
Slowly and fervently; the grots of years
Pass blindly into dust, and triumph wears
A silver splendid pathway for the river,

Whose haunts of melody grow thick, and quiver
To sound of sea deeps welcoming the end
Where thy rich glories into voices blend;
Of cadenced amethyst that never dies;
Where mortal pulses beat no agonies,
In basalt column or encrested reef,
Whose agate veins define a polished leaf,
Or marble lilies lean with slender stem,
Not moving, but just seeming to move, when
The water sways upon its pallid grace;
Turning and covering its chastened face,
While years go slowly the glaciers' pain,
And slopes are fretted in their path's moraine,
Till even glaciers break from years of sheen,
And channels burst out the firm rocks between.

Could I transfix thee with Conviction's lance
Where opaque shafts grow paler even now
What diadems were in Thought's new brow,
What noiseless tremor fading in thy flame
Might say to Doubt, "Be still," Truth is my name,
What great exact remainder might enhance
Thy weariness to grace.   The dear sad gift
A golden radiance through a night-clad rift,
Perchance the counterpart a touch would find
The strong reflection challenged thus to be
Reaction's just excess—an agony
Drawn from abysses where no line may lie,
In joys most deep, intense—Eternity—
Possess me with thy great immortal plan—
Read me the lesson of earth's little span,
The mortal measure of a day well done
On change and darkness.   The bright path alone

Ne'er lustreless, new lands break into morns,
The seed of blossoms shaken from their thorns
In rifts of Indus tremble, and grow glad;
The light illumes the good and now the bad.

  * * * * * * * * *

Oh, their prophetic right, who knew the rod
That stretched o'er deep sea ways to paths of God,
Counted the numbers that were wafted o'er
And those who never reached the further shore,
In contentions of poor human might,
When shall men name Thee and say "Here is Light ?"
By many a rock tower of the sounding deep
The vast unnumbered hosts of Pharaoh sleep;
We hear thy pulse beat in the life of Time;
We see the pillar where the serpents climb.
But where the dead sleep the strong dirge is low
With throbs of mighty sorrow in its flow.
Unmarked their crowns of youth, their burial place—
But high resplendence of thy days may trace
The isle of coral in Arabian bays!
When dates blow landward from the bending palm,
And birds seek shadows, and a place of calm—
Over them tenderly in silent hours
Blows the most wayward breath of summer flowers,
Gathering trial for a long dark fate,
Then thou art like to Isis—desolate;
But haunt, and dell, and stream, thy realm shall be
All voiceful records of thy majesty,
Without the prayer of whispers in the night;
When birds do cast no shadows in their flight, ˙
Making new harmonies grow august, when
Darkness hath gathered over hill and glen,

Fearlessness coming with a power to bless
All that were troubled in the tenderness
Of Hope, with Ægean murmurs on the strand,
Greeting new mornings on an olden land.
What though Sierras pine in vain for thee,
No crystal court hath lost its melody
Where glints of thee hath made the solitudes
Give waters from the rocks for interludes;
The eye might deem not that earthquake played
With trembling havoc in each low, hushed glade,
Whose eves so beautiful—whose limits are
Near thee and turning in the vesper star,
Hung heavenward over wastes that shall be fed—
The rock of old but for a sign hath bled,
Wherein the lion now holds sway alone,
And long white veils are draped o'er every cone.
Man's footsteps shall tread softly—and fair hands
Shall bring sweet chorded harps from other lands;
Warm lights shall from home transepts cast a glow,
And summer leaves around the casement blow,
Gently, so gently, for the human sake
Whose radiant feet shall stand nearly to break
The source of every ready sympathy;
Land of the mountain, and the sun and sea;
Most glorious presage of an altitude,
Whose allegory in thee, as a wood,
Lieth embosomed in an Island where
The sea around it cools the fervid air.

www.ingramcontent.com/pod-product-compliance
Lightning Source LLC
Chambersburg PA
CBHW032014010726
47493CB00007B/2391

* 9 7 8 3 3 3 7 3 9 1 0 5 8 *